The Night Service

TOM WALKER

CM01583054

Copyright © Tom Walker 2021.

The right of Tom Walker to be identified as the author of this work has been asserted by him in accordance with the Copyright, Designs and Patents Act, 1988.

First published in 2021 by Sharpe Books.

For my Grandad, who fought his war with courage and dignity. And never mentioned a word about it to anyone.

CONTENTS

Chapter One

The heavy rap on the door told him two things, the first was that it was that idiot Guhr who had come to fetch him. Tall, beefy, and stupid, Guhr was perfectly designed for interrogation work. That is to say, he was gifted at hurting people without killing them. *Generally*. The second was that the man in the interrogation cell upstairs had given in. It had been three days, after all.

'Herr Haupsturmfuhrer,' Guhr said, his meaty head poking incongruously around the door. 'Our guest wishes to speak with you.'

Stolcher stared wordlessly at Guhr for a moment or two, then stubbed out his cigarette in his coffee cup and rose from the heavy oak desk. Straightening his tie, he pulled his suit jacket off the hook behind the door and followed his colossus out into the hallway. They climbed the central stairwell beyond the third floor, where the signallers lived, as far as the grubby fifth floor landing. Here, a guard at a table insisted on taking his sidearm, a snub-nosed Sauer .38, and wrote his name into the visitors' log. *The administration of fear knows no bounds*, he thought to himself with a shake of his head as the log entry was completed.

Beyond the ironclad entranceway and down a dimly lit corridor, the interrogation cell door was opened for him. A smart SS man stood aside. Inside he found a pitiful example of humanity in a dirty, blood-soaked vest and trousers. It sat hunched on a wooden chair under the glare of a solitary electric light. His men had done a proper job on the prisoner. The cell floor was mopped to a shine wherever blood had been spilt; it shone everywhere.

'You wished to speak with me?'

The prisoner did not look up. He seemed to have gone beyond consciousness in some way. Eventually, he turned his face towards Stolcher. It revealed a patchwork of black bruises, swollen eyes, split lip, and a brutal gash across his forehead where he had likely been repeatedly thumped against the door. His words were hesitant and indistinct. Stolcher realised they had removed many of his teeth and even more were mere bloody stumps in his swollen mouth. He gave Guhr a withering stare.

'Go and fetch a pencil and some paper, you stupid ox.'

Guhr lumbered away and he turned back to the prisoner.

'Andre Dubreys, I know who you are. I know you served as an officer in the French Army, and I know the British call you 'Phillipe'. I know the name of the man you work for, and that of the man *he* works for. I also know your job is to identify grounds suitable for parachutists and organise welcoming committees. I knew all of these things before you even opened your mouth - so you might wonder what it is that I need from you now?'

Dubreys stared at him wordlessly through his devastated face. It was the face of a man who had been awake ever since he had been rolled up in a raid on his safehouse by the Gestapo three days ago. He had been chained to a radiator and woken whenever he looked like he was going to fall asleep. The beatings did not actually begin until the second day, but when they came, they were relentless. As was the shouting and the questioning, alternating in German and French. This was by no means the first interrogation Stolcher had overseen and he knew every prisoner began the process believing themselves to be strong. That was why he never bothered even attending the first day of an interrogation. Very few lasted beyond the second day, however, and Dubreys had done well to make it to the morning of day three.

Stolcher's irritation stemmed from the length of time he had managed to hold out. Only because it had undoubtedly given others the opportunity to escape. Now he was anxious to get on with his plan, long in formulation and much refined. Guhr returned with writing materials. He stood awkwardly for a man of such impressive girth and brutal nature, looking to Stolcher for instructions.

'Well, find a table and put them on it,' Stolcher told him, impatiently. Turning back to the prisoner he spoke in a neutral voice, the closest he ever came to sounding warm.

'What I want from you are the locations of your landing grounds for both parachutists and aircraft. I want your escape routes and procedures, the names of all the people involved in the organisation of supplying the resistance, and the names of all your contacts in British military intelligence. And finally, I want your ciphers. Write it all down now, in detail and omit nothing. If you do this quickly, I will speak to my boss about bringing a doctor here to look at your wounds and you will receive food and water. *Verstehen*?' Stolcher cursed inwardly as he inadvertently drifted into German from his otherwise flawless French.

With the writing materials on the table before him, Dubreys looked somehow even more wretched. His face betrayed him. He would spill everything, Stolcher concluded with satisfaction. The prisoner picked up the pencil with his right hand. It was the one they had, thankfully, remembered not to break any of the fingers on. The fingernails on this grubby hand had been torn out though. It left bloody marks on the paper as he wrote. The letters were distorted and ugly, like his face.

'I will return in one hour, to check on your progress, and I will bring a physician,' Stolcher said. As he passed the SS man in the corridor he stopped and spoke to him quietly, 'You can tell Ritteln that Operation BALDUR is now active.'

'Jawohl, Herr Hauptsturmfuhrer. And the prisoner?'

Stolcher glanced over his shoulder and lowered his voice further, ‘Bring his notes to me when he’s finished. Then shoot him and throw his body in the river.’

Chapter Two

Crete, May 1941

The whip-crack of rifle fire echoed across the aerodrome from the crude range north of RAF Heraklion's main runway, overlooking the sea. It was the only sound disturbing the otherwise still morning air. It rebounded back to the firing point from the high ground to the south, where the radar station stood alone on Ames Ridge. The sea sparkled in the spring sunshine just a little way off beyond the targets, a bunch of empty oil drums.

Greece had fallen, Rommel was advancing across North Africa, and here in the Eastern Mediterranean an invasion of Crete was expected any day. Although, if that fact conferred a sense of urgency on the island's defenders, it was not apparent to the firers. It certainly made no difference to their accuracy, in Charlie Kendrick's somewhat jaundiced view. A 22-year old veteran of the campaigns in Egypt and Greece, Kendrick would rather be just about anywhere other than here. He had already fought the Germans and the Italians in the air and couldn't foresee a scenario in which he would need to meet them in ground combat. His Station Commander's directive that all remaining RAF personnel should be trained to repulse an aerodrome attack seemed a waste of time and an unhelpful diversion from the real business of fighting the war.

Kendrick gripped the Thompson sub-machine gun tightly and squinted down the sights. An oil drum wavered indistinctly at the end of the barrel. He closed his left eye and snatched the trigger. The weapon jerked, surprising him with its mechanical hammering as it sprayed a quantity of bullets at random. He lowered the gun and studied the drum from afar. There was not a single hole in it; nor any sign of where the other rounds had gone. He shook his head. It was a terrible result from only 30 yards away.

'Mr Kendrick, sir, that was bloody awful. I've seen some terrible shots in my time, yes I have, but you take the bleedin' biscuit. If you can't shoot an oil drum from this distance, how do you expect to hit a Jerry paratrooper when he comes running at you?'

Sergeant Roskilly had appeared close to apoplexy all morning, but this display of incompetence pushed him over the edge. The stocky Yorkshireman came steaming down the firing line and took the weapon out of Charlie's sweaty hands with an insistent tug.

'I thought it was *your* job to shoot the Nazi paratroopers for me, Sergeant,' Charlie replied with a smile. There was some snickering along the line.

'What are you lot staring at? Carry on. Mr Denhay - use both hands on that pistol please.'

Roskilly spoke in a voice loud enough to be heard on the other side of the airfield. Charlie flicked his friend and pilot, Peter Denhay, a knowing glance. Peter grinned back, clearly enjoying his discomfort.

'I know this a big joke for you, sir. But you know who else thinks this is a joke?'

Charlie shook his head wordlessly, sensing a trap.

'Jerry, that's who. See, he don't drop with his weapon, so he needs a few seconds to sort himself out before he can fight. It stands to reason that you have an immediate advantage if you can shoot straight. But the way *you* shoot, he could sit down and have his tea before you get anywhere near him. Now give it another go.'

Charlie took the weapon back, his face reddened at the Sergeant's words. He pulled the butt into his shoulder and gripped it tightly again, concentrating on the target.

'Don't grip too hard. Firm pressure. Brace your supporting elbow against your chest. Measure your breathing and fire on the outward breath.' Roskilly said quietly.

Charlie tucked his supporting arm in and let the air slip out of his lungs. The drum appeared in the centre of his sights. He gently squeezed the trigger. The Thompson gave a metallic burp and he looked over the sights at the target.

'Three hits on target. We'll make a soldier out of you yet, sir,' Roskilly said without a smile and moved onto the next man. Charlie noticed the weapon's working parts were locked to the rear, showing an empty chamber. He released the empty magazine and was just about to head over to the ammunition point when an Austin staff car pulled up. A khaki-clad RAF officer climbed out and walked purposefully over. He waited a moment or two out of respect for Sergeant Roskilly's instruction before addressing them in a formal tone.

'Denhay and Kendrick. The Station Commander needs to see you both. Now.'

Charlie laid his Thompson down, shielded his eyes from the sun and addressed the unknown officer, 'What's the Old Man want with us?'

'Damned if I know, old chap. Maybe they're posting you to Bomber Command? Out of the frying pan, eh?'

Charlie didn't smile. In his experience, it was exactly the sort of thing the RAF was capable of.

*

Peter Denhay adjusted his tatty forage cap in the mirror outside the Station Commander's office and studied his face. He was thinner than he remembered. His mahogany skin, a product of several weeks spent under a Cretan sun, made him look older than he actually was, and he pulled a serious face.

'Quit posing, you still look devastatingly handsome,' Charlie said with chuckle. He'd entered the corridor quietly and caught Peter admiring himself.

'I was just checking my hat,' Peter lied.

The door swung inwards and the Station Commander told them to enter. He looked hot and harassed in his service dress uniform and greeted them civilly, but absently. Peter had more than a little sympathy for Wing Commander Brown because he had much on his mind today. He had only been commanding RAF Heraklion for two months, and most of his people were the sweepings of the units that had survived the catastrophe in Greece. He was short on supplies and had insufficient aircraft to defend the skies above Crete during the impending battle. Much lower down on the list was what to do with a single lost Blenheim crew that he had inherited. But Brown now addressed this with the same gusto he applied to his many other problems.

'I have some bad news I'm afraid chaps. It's been impossible to locate your squadron,' Brown said. Peter was unsurprised. Everything he had learned about the RAF in his short period of service so far told him this would happen.

'There was some hope that they had been sent to the Sudan, or Iraq,' Brown continued, 'But the whole picture is a damned mess currently. It's order, counter-order, disorder.'

'That's alright, sir. We thought they might have been disbanded after Greece, so we're very happy to stay on here and help with the defence,' Peter said. Out of the corner of his eye he saw Charlie look upwards at the ceiling and he ignored it.

Brown cleared his throat.

'I can't really see how I can put a light bomber to good use in the coming battle. The Germans won't get a foothold here so-'

Brown trailed off. There was a short silence as Peter pondered how best to make his protest.

'Well we've been attacking shipping for the last few weeks, sir. And, Charlie will agree, we've got rather good at our low-level attacks, haven't we?

Charlie nodded unenthusiastically.

Brown looked doubtful. His eyes flicked to a signal on his desk and back to Peter.

'I hear all that, but it's all decided. I asked Cairo for some orders for you and they told me "there are Blenheims on Malta, send 'em there", they said.'

'Malta, sir? But what about Crete – you'll need every aircraft you can lay your hands on when the Germans make their move,' Peter replied. He had seen the speed the Germans moved at in Greece and was surprised that Brown should intend to reduce the size of his air force at this critical point.

Brown gave Peter a searching look and sighed, 'I dare say you're right. But,' Brown waved the signal at them, 'Orders are orders. And yours are to make your way to Malta. Today. Is that understood?'

Brown's tone was firm and unequivocal. They replied in unison.

'Sir.'

'Good. I'll signal Valetta to let them know you're on your way. You can take some bombs with you too – save us blowing them up. That way you can have a crack at Jerry if the opportunity presents,' Brown smiled. He looked relieved as he stood, indicating their interview was over. Peter saluted smartly. Charlie touched his hand to his hat.

'Best of luck chaps. Fair winds and all that.'

'And to you, sir,' Peter replied.

*

‘I can’t see why you look so glum at the thought of getting off this godforsaken rock,’ Charlie said, shaking his head. ‘We’re swapping one island for another in my view. And both are damned bad deals.’

Peter was staring out of the Austin’s window at the scrubby grass and stony earth of the airfield and he replied without looking back at his navigator.

‘I feel like we’re skipping out on this before the climax. It feels-’ Peter searched for the words, ‘-un-British.’

‘There’s nothing more British than quitting before it’s all over, Peter. Just look at the way we’ve fought this war,’ Charlie replied.

Peter turned angrily on Charlie and snapped, ‘It’s not a laughing matter. Why can’t you just take this seriously for once?’

Charlie looked chastened. He fell silent and said nothing more for the entire journey to the dispersal. As they arrived, Peter saw that the servicing crew loaned to them from 112 Squadron had their aircraft bombed-up and ready to fly. Q-Queen, known as *Queenie* to her crew, was a long-nosed Bristol Blenheim Mark IV that had seen service in Egypt and had been saved from destruction in Greece. Despite a shortage of spares and tools, the engineers had managed to keep the aircraft serviceable for the past few weeks, caring for it as they did their own Gloucester Gladiator fighters.

In the fierce light of the forenoon it was difficult to see quite how much she was marked from her operational history, but Peter knew the scars were there. Dirty black marks on the engine nacelles around the exhausts, bullet holes taped up, and an ugly, jagged patch repair on one wing where a caique-mounted anti-aircraft gun had very nearly done for them on one anti-shipping sortie.

Climbing out of the car, Peter steeled himself for another difficult conversation he knew he had to have. Corporal Carew greeted them wearing his parachute harness.

'Afternoon, sir. She's all topped up and ready for the off. What's the plan today?'

Charlie caught Peter's eye in passing and he made a face that said, *rather you than me.*

'Carew, there's no easy way to say this. We've got our marching orders and we're to take the kite off to Malta. We won't be coming back, so this is goodbye for now. We'll miss having a gunner like you,' Peter said, adopting a certain stiff tone.

Carew looked disappointed. He'd been flying as their temporary air gunner for the last few weeks because their actual gunner had been killed in Greece. Carew was not a qualified air gunner and was only on loan because 112 Squadron had fewer aeroplanes than normal. It was clear to Peter that the Corporal considered himself part of their crew now.

'I don't suppose there's any hope of speaking to my boss to get permission to come along. You'll need an air gunner wherever you go.'

'I'm sorry, it just won't do. Thank you for everything, you've been a real champ in the turret.' Peter needed to be firm, he felt wretched enough as it was leaving everyone in the lurch like this. He hadn't the courage for a long, drawn out discussion. He gripped the crestfallen man's hand and turned away immediately, throwing his small canvas bag up onto the wing before climbing up to the cockpit. Charlie was already strapped in and looking over the map marked with the route to Malta.

'How'd he take it?'

'Alright, I guess,' Peter grunted.

They started up wordlessly and, waving farewell to the engineers, taxied out to the runway threshold and took off into the clear, blue sky. Their route ran due west over the tip of Crete and out over the Mediterranean, just over 600 solid miles to Malta. Peter climbed up to 15, 000 feet where they had an uninterrupted view of 150 miles of empty sea in every direction. With the aircraft trimmed and set for the cruise, he had time to ponder his own mood.

Something felt wrong. He knew himself well enough to be certain of that. His disappointment at being sent away from Greece was only part of a wider problem. He sensed it was equal parts a belief that he was not doing enough to help win the war, and an emptiness caused by the loss of the woman he loved. At least he thought he loved her. Although he had spent only a matter of hours with Eve Moore, her parting kiss on a windswept field in northern Greece had left him unable to think about anyone else.

'Smoke, nine o'clock low,' Charlie said in an indifferent voice.

The news broke into Peter's private thoughts and dragged him back to the situation at hand. He wondered how long he had been day-dreaming. Smoke could only come from a ship. The question was: whose ship?

Peter eased the aircraft into a gentle turn towards the black smudge on the horizon. He let the altitude bleed off as they approached and they were a little over 2,000 feet by the time it resolved itself into a clearly defined object.

'It's a steamer, I reckon about 1,500 tons or thereabouts. No escort. Italian, I guess, by its course,' Charlie said from the nose where he had gone to get a better look.

'All the way out here? That's quite some detour from the Libyan ports. They must be under a lot of pressure,' Peter replied. He glanced down at the ship as it passed under the wing out of sight. He thought nothing of the risk of attacking a blockade runner. They'd taken on more formidable targets than this. He tightened his straps and called, 'Alright Charlie, brace for the attack run. Tally ho, tally ho.'

The descent to 50 feet, which was below mast height, took an instant and soon they were hammering along at 240 mph towards the ship. Their suspicions were confirmed when a couple of gun emplacements exploded into life, sending tracer fire arcing towards them. Peter nimbly side-stepped the fire by jinking the aircraft and, as the ship loomed towards them, he suddenly realised how big it really was. He just about made out the name *Lorotino* on the starboard bow, when he heard Charlie's shout on the intercom, 'Bomb's gone.'

Peter pulled back violently, in the knowledge that it was necessary to both 'skip' the bombs towards the target and put distance between the aircraft and the resultant explosion. They were over in a flash and a tremendous explosion beneath them seemed to lift the aeroplane bodily for a moment before they descended again on the other side.

'She's smoking amidships. Christ-'

Hearing Charlie stop mid-sentence, Peter glanced about until his gaze landed on their starboard engine, which was burning fiercely. He'd landed a crippled bomber with one engine flaming before, but he didn't recall the flames being that intense.

'Ditch it, before the fuel tank goes up,' Charlie shouted as he buckled his harness. Without another thought, Peter closed the throttle and let the aircraft nose-down towards the sea. At this reduced altitude he saw that the surface, which had appeared calm and undisturbed higher up, was actually really choppy. It was too late to do anything about that now, he decided. He tightened his straps, a precaution he had forgotten once before and had paid the price with a broken nose. The water rose to meet them, mottled blue and green. Peter held the control column back, feeling the airspeed bleed off the aeroplane as it approached the inevitable stalling point.

With an enormous splash, the Blenheim nosed in. Water immediately rushed up and over the cockpit, blotting out the sun for a moment and giving the impression that they were underwater. But, like an improbable buff and brown whale, *Queenie* surfaced again, her fires extinguished by gallons of sea water. Water rushed into the cockpit and it filled quickly. With the sigh of escaping air, she sank below the waves.

*

When seen from its normal perspective, which is to say from shore looking seaward, the sea can often appear refreshing, inviting even. But viewed from the perspective of a life raft floating upon its surface, quite out of sight of land, it gains a terrifyingly isolated quality. To be stranded at sea, Peter reflected, is to truly know how feeble one compares to the might of capricious nature.

Tossed about in their yellow rubber three-man dingy, they were an insignificant speck on a broad seascape that stretched away to the endless horizon in all directions. They were together, but together they were alone. Even the temporary security of their present precarious situation was not guaranteed to last. But though it did not seem like it, they had a great deal to be thankful for, since *Queenie's* rapid descent to the seabed had very nearly consumed them both. As they drifted listlessly, Peter dreamed of their escape from the stricken aircraft.

The weight pressing down on the sliding canopy hatch had made it impossible to open and the cockpit filled with icy cold water as the aircraft sank. Peter had heard Charlie's desperate warning that he was opening the gunner's hatch as his head submerged. The hatch swung inward to admit hundreds of gallons of cold salt water into the fuselage. This at least gave them a way out.

In the darkening cockpit Peter took a final breath, released his straps and groped his way towards the escape hatch. He was blind but found it by touch and tried to pull himself through, when a tug at his waist stopped him dead. The ties of his Mae West were caught around something. Grasping at it with his fingers made no difference; he wanted to scream out. His lungs burned with effort of containing the rapidly diminishing oxygen. The aircraft continued to sink. Peter felt the light beyond the surface fading. Oddly, the panic drained from his body and his energy to resist went with it. He relaxed and was ready to accept death.

Then hands tore at his life jacket, undoing the ties and helping him out. He felt suddenly free and rose, slowly at first. Up he went, up towards the light and the warmer water. It was an awfully long time before his head broke the surface and he took a lungful of fresh air, close to the inflated dingy.

'Nearly lost you there,' Charlie spluttered, backstroking towards the life raft with all the care of a Serpentine bather. He clambered into the raft and then helped Peter aboard. He collapsed in the bottom in an ungainly heap, wheezing and coughing. When he regained his senses, he lay for a moment without speaking and just listened to the sound of the waves lapping against their little craft.

'Looks like a successful hit,' Charlie said, pointing to the smudge of grey smoke on the horizon, the only evidence the steamer ever existed.

'On both accounts, perhaps,' Peter eventually managed to say with the beginnings of a wry smile.

Charlie opened a watertight survival bag and laid out the contents. There was a pack containing 72 hours' worth of dehydrated rations, a fishing kit, water purification tablets sealed in a greased wrapper, a survival knife with a blunt tip, a packet of dingy stoppers, some boiled sweets, and a tin containing Benzedrine Sulphate tablets.

'We should organise ourselves,' Peter said, blinking salt water from his eyes. 'Two-hour watches: one sleeps while the other keeps lookout or does chores. The secret to survival at sea is routine. Do you have a map on you?'

'No, it was in the aircraft.'

'What do you think our chances are of getting picked up out here?'

'We never got an emergency call off, so it's unlikely they'll come looking for us. I reckon we were about 100 miles due east of Crete when we spotted the steamer; we can't be too far off a convoy route.'

'Something will come,' Peter agreed with a sickening twinge of despair.

What came was a storm. They watched it build all through the remainder of that first day. By the time the sun touched the horizon the wind whistled above their heads so loud it felt to Peter like his eardrums would burst. Soon the waves formed great peaks around them, the tops of which were torn off and sent flying by the strong breeze. The salt spray stung his eyes and he prayed for a break from sea water, regretting when it came in great heavy drops of rain out of the dark sky. In total darkness the only way to tell whether he was drenched by sea or sky was the taste of the water in his mouth.

At first, they fought to do all in their power to maintain the dingy's buoyancy. So, while Charlie laid out plastic bags to collect drinking water, Peter bailed out furiously with his flying boot. But the constant motion of the boat was debilitating and both men soon became exhausted. An enormous wave swamped the dingy and snatched away the half-filled bags of rainwater, the fishing kit, and the survival knife. Peter felt so seasick he could not care less about their lost equipment. Drowning would be a kindness at this point, he decided as he dry retched again over the side. His body told him his stomach was empty.

The weak morning sun found them laid like drowned rats in the bottom of the dingy, which rose and fell with the waves, now much-diminished in height. Peter awoke in a pool of lukewarm seawater and the flotsam of the survival kit. Charlie's sleeping head was laid on his shoulder. He was amazed they had survived the night's ordeal. Had the dingy gone over at any point they would have gone into the sea. In their reduced state it would have been unlikely that either man could right and regain the life raft, for to fail to do so would be to succumb to either hypothermia or secondary drowning.

The passing of the storm really only improved their situation by a fraction because now their drinking water was gone, as was their means of feeding themselves once the rations were consumed. Peter munched on a brown biscuit and followed it with a couple of the Benzedrine tablets for good measure. Shortly afterwards he felt an unexpected improvement in his mood.

'Wake up, Charlie. What a fine day. Isn't it smashing that we're alive?'

Charlie opened one eye cautiously and groaned, 'What's wrong with you? Why are you smiling like that?'

'I'm just relieved that we've survived our first night at sea. It's a good omen.'

Charlie sat up, blinking in the bright sunshine, and studied Peter.

'Is it? Captain Bligh had to sail 4,000 miles in an open boat. Was it a good omen for him?'

The following days were long and uncomfortable. Occasionally they talked, once they sang. Increasingly, they sat in silence. They moved about to try to relieve their discomfort and experimented with different techniques for gathering water.

Eventually finding they could make enough to wet their tongues by evaporation. The sun climbed to its zenith, subjecting them to the intensity of its merciless rays. Then it dropped away leaving them shivering in their damp, salty clothes throughout the night. On the third night they thought they heard a whale calling and then an aeroplane, high up above them heading towards Africa away to the south. Neither event made a material difference to their odds of rescue and their hopes diminished in consequence.

On the morning of the fourth day, Charlie was dividing the rations out and Peter was slumped over the side with his shirt over his head. They did not talk; they could not talk because they were so parched. Peter saw the motorboat first, but when he opened his mouth his voice was barely audible. Charlie looked up from the rations to Peter and then on to the boat at which he pointed. It was a couple of miles off and making a turn away from them.

Charlie knelt up in the raft and removed his shirt, which he waved frantically above his head. The boat continued its turn away from them and headed off on an easterly course. Peter cradled his head in his hands because it was obvious they would be abandoned. But then it made an unexpected turn back towards them. It threw white water either side of its bow, a thin strip of black waterline showed where it parted the waves.

Peter tried to speak but the words caught in his throat. Charlie gripped his arm. He was crying, although no tears rolled down his face. As the vessel came alongside, sailors reached down to help them up onto the deck. Here, Peter noticed for the first time the two torpedoes either side of the flying bridge, and the green, white, and red ensign of the Italian Navy. An officer approached them with a canteen of water that he offered as the crew helped them onto the boat.

'Gentlemen, I am *Sottotenente di Vascallo* Enzo Beretta, commander of this motor torpedo boat. I regret to say you are our prisoners.'

*

Beretta was, like most Italians in Charlie's estimation, entirely harmless. A short and jolly chap, he saw to their immediate needs of refreshment and gave them full and free movement aboard his ship, in return for their promise not to attempt escape. Charlie glanced about him at miles of empty water and laughed.

Beretta explained that he expected to return to port within 24 hours. His mission was to search for a missing auxiliary cruiser, but they had turned up no signs at all. Charlie said nothing about the *Lorotino* but caught Peter's eye and gave him a significant look.

Being in the life raft for such a long period had taken a toll on them. Peter slept for 10 hours straight, wrapped in a blanket in a wooden bunk in the forepeak. His body was cruelly ravaged by the experience, with salt rash around his armpits and legs, and severe sunburn. He needed time to heal. But Charlie bounced back much quicker. He made a point of eating whatever the crew put in front of him and spent as much time as possible on deck, hoping to catch sight of a British vessel. Late in the afternoon, he got lucky.

'Psst, Peter. Are you awake there?'

The dying afternoon light filtered down the companionway, filling the cabin with its soft glow. The sound of the boat's engine grew louder and somehow more urgent.

'What time is it?'

'It's just gone 1700 hours. You've been out for the count.'

'How long before we land? I'm bloody sick of this now. I shan't ever go to sea again.'

'For God's sake, Peter, shut up and listen to me. The Wops have spotted a ship to the north. They're turning away now to avoid him, but they're all spooked by it.'

He led Peter onto deck, still wrapped in his blanket. Other than the rating at the helm, the crew of the motor torpedo boat stared quietly over to the north-east, where a light cruiser was hull-up on the horizon. It was making steam to intercept them, which forced Beretta to run a westerly course to avoid him, taking them further away from their home port.

Beretta spotted them and strolled over. If he was worried about the unknown vessel, it did not register on his tanned face and he beamed a broad white-toothed grin.

'He is one of yours, *si*?'

'You tell me,' Charlie shrugged. 'You're the sailor.'

'*Si*, *si*. A Dido Class, no?'

They said nothing, but Beretta didn't seem to mind. Dido Class or not, he knew he had 15 knots over him and, short of an absolute disaster, they would leave the cruiser far behind before nightfall. Beretta shouted something to the crew of the rear-mounted heavy machine gun, and they laughed. In very little time the cruiser was only visible from its smoke over the horizon. The crew relaxed noticeably, and some were sent below to fix the evening meal. Beretta gave orders to the helmsman to maintain their westerly course until nightfall and then double back towards Italy.

Charlie felt hope itself dying, and the sight of the cruiser slipping away behind them was like seeing it sewed into its hammock and dropped into the water. He wondered what life in an Italian prisoner of war camp would be like and hoped it would be better than what the chaps in Germany had to contend with. The colour of the sea changed to a deep dark blue as the sun set. The sky reddened in the west and, other than Charlie who remained in a deep funk, the remaining men on deck gazed at it with some satisfaction.

An explosion off to port sent a white fountain of water high into the air, startling everyone. Charlie physically jumped, instinctively thinking they had struck a mine. Beretta appeared on deck with a pair of binoculars and scanned the horizon. Another explosion, closer still. Covering his eyes, Peter saw that three more light cruisers were coming up fast from the west. The dipping sun had covered their approach, enabling them to get within a few miles of the torpedo boat undetected. Their pursuer had done an excellent job of shepherding the fast boat into the waiting cruisers. It was a clever trap.

Beretta looked around at his crew, who searched his face in anticipation of orders. The next round would not be a warning, he knew. Charlie could see he was weighing up his options: fight or flee. Another round landed just beyond the bow. It exploded, sending water high into the air, but the blast caught a young rating on the foredeck gun and tore him apart. Charlie felt something strike his head and then found himself laid on the deck with blood running down his face. He was completely unaware of what had hit him, but Peter was bending over him and trying to mop up the blood with his blanket. Charlie's head throbbed and his right eye was blinded, but he saw Beretta step forward to the helm and draw back the throttles to bring the boat to a standstill. Her headway gone, she rolled gently on the swell.

Fifteen minutes later, a Royal Navy motor launch drew alongside under the command of a sub-lieutenant with a boarding party of sailors in tropical uniform. Their tanned faces peered across betraying a mixture of curiosity and scepticism, an encounter with this enemy at this range was something of a novelty. The naval officer announced loudly to all on deck that he intended to take possession of the vessel and that all crew were to relinquish their stations and move aft. He repeated the order again in English, but much louder this time. All complied with the order, except Charlie and Peter who sat amidships looking like a pair of tramps.

'Did you not hear me?' The young man addressed them impatiently, 'I said all crew to go aft. Stupid bloody dagos.'

'We're not crew,' replied Peter. 'And we're certainly not dagos.'

Chapter Three

'Hauptsturmfuhrer Stolcher.' The orderly announced in a formal voice, holding the door open. Putting down his fountain pen and looking up from the mess of files across his desk, Ritteln watched him enter. Stolcher was short with a long nose and sparse hair, slicked across his head in the way that was popular amongst some of the younger men. The only remarkable thing about him, Ritteln decided, was his piercing grey eyes that seemed to lack any warmth whatsoever.

Stolcher clicked his heels together and gave a smart Nazi salute, which Ritteln returned with a casual wave. This might have appeared disrespectful to the Fuhrer, if one did not know that Standartenfuhrer Werner Ritteln was Head of Internal Security for the Reich Main Security Office, or R.H.S.A., in occupied France.

'Sit down, Stolcher, please.'

He gestured to a couple of deep leather armchairs positioned before his imposing mahogany desk. The office was on the third floor of the R.H.S.A.'s headquarters on Avenue Foch and light flooded in through large windows that overlooked the wide boulevard running down to the Arc de Triomphe. It illuminated a room decorated in the highest possible fashion.

'Welcome to Paris,' Ritteln smiled. 'I think you will find it somewhat different to your previous appointment in…,' he cast about looking for a file in the chaotic mess of paper on his desk.

'Poland, sir. I was in Lublin,' Stolcher removed an envelope from his jacket pocket, his letter of recommendation. Leaning forward, he placed it on Ritteln's desk. Ritteln opened the envelope and drew out the letter within, putting on a pair of wire-rimmed spectacles to read. Stolcher sat quietly as his credentials were scrutinised.

Ritteln removed his glasses and frowned, 'I see that Globocnik thought highly of you. You're the fellow they call *Der Jude Jager* aren't you? Globocnik states you were instrumental in setting up the Jewish Quarter in Lublin. He calls you "Ruthless".'

Stolcher flashed a humourless smile and spoke in his high-pitched voice, 'Herr Globocnik was kind enough to take my advice on matters of counter-intelligence. Before the R.H.S.A., I was with the SiPo and trained in detective work, surveillance and interrogation. I believe that my particular skills may be of use to you here.'

The *Sicherheitspolizei* or SiPo were the secret state police force that included the Gestapo.

'This will be a promotion for you then,' Ritteln smiled. 'I'm not fond of social climbers, you know. And Globocnik may be unaware that France is not considered to be thick with enemy plots. I personally consider it to be something of a backwater when it comes to national resistance activities,' Ritteln said dismissively.

'And I aim to ensure that it remains that way, Herr Standartenfuhrer.'

Ritteln blinked, wondering if this ass had actually just said that. He stared angrily and looked like he'd been punched in the gut.

'One might question whether it is advisable to question your superior's effectiveness on your first day in the office,' he said eventually.

Stolcher shifted in his seat.

'I meant no criticism, Herr Standartenfuhrer. But I have an idea I wanted to share with you, and that was why I asked for this meeting. I think it will be of great interest to you and has the potential to enhance your standing within the R.H.S.A. several times over.'

Ritteln exploded.

'What the fuck makes you think my standing needs any enhancement?'

He was on his feet now. His fists clenched and his fat face turning an ugly shade of purple up to his bald pate, which retained its original corpse-white colour.

Stolcher sat calmly in the face of this tirade. In the hierarchy of Reich security organisations, Werner Ritteln was an immensely powerful man. He only had to say the word and people were rounded up and shot or disappeared. Like some vast spider, he sat at the centre of a web of intelligence that extended across all of France, and beyond. He was a humourless man unused to being questioned.

'I have developed a plan that aims to ruin nascent British intelligence networks in France and discredit national resistance indefinitely,' Stolcher said.

In the silence that followed Ritteln regained his seat.

'Tell me more,' he said, adopting a more nonchalant tone of voice.

Stolcher reached for his attaché case and withdrew a folder marked with the Reichsadler, it had the title 'Operation BALDUR' written on the front.

'What would you say if I told you it was possible to throw British intelligence into disarray to such an extent that they won't just lose faith in the French, but will also cause them to mistrust themselves?'

'I'm listening.'

'The aim of Operation BALDUR is to deceive the British by carefully growing an intelligence network that exists entirely under our control. If we do it right, the required investment will be insignificant. In fact, the British will pay for it themselves in people and resources.'

Ritteln considered this for a moment.

'I see you've named it after a Norse god. You don't worry that the inference will give away the nature of the operation?'

Baldur was the son of Odin and Frigg. Supposedly immortal, his demise had come about from a seemingly innocuous sprig of mistletoe.

'The British will never come to know the name of the operation,' Stolcher replied blandly.

'I'm intrigued. How do you propose to bait them?'

'We'll use real gold; we'll feed them details of a classified project. We just limit the quantity so they remain tantalised, but can never establish a full picture.'

'Can't we fabricate something? We could dream up a project close enough to believe but is, ultimately, a facade.'

'The plan hinges on the British being able to independently verify the intelligence, so that it reinforces their own preconceptions. If we offer something unexpected, they will treat it with caution. Ultimately, it could make the difference between success and failure.'

'I see,' Ritteln said, looking displeased. 'I'll need to clear this all through Berlin, of course.'

'Of course, Herr Standartenfuhrer. If I may, I would stipulate with Berlin that whatever we offer must be of sufficient interest to excite the British. It cannot be economic reports or studies into the labour crisis.'

'Very well. Now tell me more about the specifics of the plan, so that I can explain it in detail to my superiors.'

Stolcher smiled. He explained the rules of the game in simple terms and Ritteln listened, asking the occasional question. It was no secret that the British desired to develop latent resistance across occupied Europe into active networks. The Germans had achieved some modest success in disrupting their attempts and the R.H.S.A. assessment of the state of intelligence and sabotage operations in France in 1941 seemed reasonable. It was assessed to be highly localised, tribal, and disorganised.

The key to Operation BALDUR, Stolcher told him, was keeping the British convinced that their fake network was viable. They would start by capturing a couple of agents, then use their wireless to summon more. By alluding to acts of sabotage and reporting nuggets of phoney intelligence, they would deliberately build a circuit that could be used to deceive the British into believing their disinformation. As it grew, it would subsume smaller networks of genuine agents until, at a point yet to be determined, Stolcher would give a signal and everyone would be rounded up. The game would eventually be revealed to the British, but it would be too late to save their agents. Stolcher estimated BALDUR would set British spying back years. Perhaps for good.

'They will be back to 1939 again, and then some,' Stolcher said, gleefully.

Ritteln sat back in his chair and looked thoughtful.

'How can you be sure they'll fall for it? The British are the past masters of deception, they might play us at our own game.'

'That's easy, I have someone on the inside.'

'What?' Ritteln was stunned by this news. Members of the R.H.S.A. were not authorised to run intelligence agents without strict approval from higher authority; it was highly irregular.

'Have you reported this to anyone other than me?'

'No.'

'Who is it?'

'I think it wise for your sake and mine if I decline to answer that. But I can tell you they have been in my pocket since before Munich and they sit right at the heart of London's intelligence gathering apparatus.' Stolcher looked pleased with this twist. If

Ritteln didn't know about the double-agent then he retained plausible deniability.

Ritteln grunted.

'Leave the file. I want to reflect on it overnight,' he said finally.

Stolcher stood and flung a final salute.

'Sieg heil.'

Ritteln waved him away. As he reached the door, Ritteln spoke.

'Oh, Stolcher?'

He turned back towards the desk. Ritteln did not look up from the mass of papers and his scribbled notes.

'If you try to fuck me over this, I'll send you to some place so dark and miserable that you'll dream of working in ghettos again.'

*

As far as nondescript boardrooms went, the one at 64 Baker Street was bog-standard. If its high ceilings and faded stucco had any stories to tell, they were lost to time. Georgian sash windows peered out onto the busy street below, admitting a modest light into the otherwise bare-walled room. The windows were cracked open, it being June, and with the light also came the noise from below. Taxis and buses rattled by, workmen down the street were loudly clearing what remained of the offices of a bombed-out underwriter.

The sign outside the boardroom advertised it as a meeting of the Inter-Services Research Bureau, but the bland title belied the importance of what was taking place beyond the soundproof door. For this was actually a routine conference of the Operations Division of the Special Operations Executive, or S.O.E., and its purpose was to plan how to set Europe ablaze. Or at least that was the intent, thought Lieutenant Colonel James

Sutherland (Jumbo to his few friends) who attended in his capacity as liaison officer to S.O.E.

Aside from a few small set piece operations on the continent, the S.O.E. had barely registered an effect on the course of the war. Sutherland judged the organisation to be, at best, a negligible quantity and, at worst, a dangerous nuisance that was costly and politically dangerous. He should know, since Sutherland had over 25 years' spying experience. This experience told him the multiple objectives of S.O.E., to conduct espionage, gather intelligence, and raise secret armies, were contradictory. It was a contradiction that did not sit easily with him, because S.O.E. was poaching on his own organisation's territory.

Most of the dozen or so people sat around the long oak conference table wore military uniform. Overwhelmingly represented were the various shades of khaki service dress denoting officers of the army. Most regiments and corps could be seen: several guardsmen; a gunner; two engineers; and a chap from the Royal Army Service Corps, although he was taking the minutes.

At the head of the table sat a Brigadier, the Head of Operations, who chaired this meeting. The others were the section heads for the staff branches running agents in occupied Europe. Their operations stretched from the Atlantic to the Baltic and touched almost everywhere in between. The Head was a tall, lithe man with a greying moustache, which he stroked unconsciously as he scribbled in a notebook in green ink.

The man speaking now headed up F-Section, one of the bodies responsible for France. He was a major in the Royal Regiment of Artillery although, like many of the other attendees, he was not a career soldier. His thick glasses and well-polished accent hinted at this. Before the formation of S.O.E., Sutherland had learned, he had been a professor of modern history at Oxford. Many of the others had also been recruited into the organisation for their specialist skills. They referred to themselves as 'The Baker Street Irregulars' or joked that they worked at 'The Ministry of Ungentlemanly Warfare'. Sutherland reflected that you could tell a lot about people by the names they picked for themselves; in the best British tradition, they were amateurs.

'And so, I can confidently predict that we will have established a network of something approaching 300 agents between Lorient and Paris before the end of the year,' Major Ivor Jones said, closing the buff file and removing his spectacles to stare at the Head in his inimitable style.

Sutherland cleared his throat. It was the first noise he had emitted in the 55 minutes since the meeting started, and both the Head and Jones turned to look at him.

'May I ask what level of confidence you have in the information provided by your network? Forgive me, I didn't catch the name you used.'

'Grapple? The Grapple network is one of our finest sources of information in northern France, presently,' Jones replied in a patronising tone. 'It was their handiwork on the Lorient-Tours line that prevented essential U-boat components from reaching the dockyards last month.'

Sutherland considered this statement, which he knew to be only partly true. There had been congestion on the Lorient-Tours line, but his own sources told him it had not resulted in any demonstrable effect on U-boat operations at Lorient, nor anywhere else for that matter. He said nothing in response.

'No, I have utmost faith in Grapple. Its information is gold dust,' Jones concluded with a weak smile.

'That's rather my point. In my experience of intelligence work, the things that sound too good to be true often are just that. Just look at your casualty figures-'

'Grapple has had no casualties.'

'Exactly. You've been running this network for months and yet you've had no agents killed, none taken prisoner, and none forced to use an escape line. How does that compare with your other sections?'

The Head leaned forward in his chair and addressed Sutherland in a gruff voice, 'Let's not cover that here. Do you have any specific information from your organisation that would lead us to question the veracity of the Grapple network?'

Sutherland had nothing he wished to add at this time. That is to say, he had no evidence or facts on which to base the hypothesis now forming in his mind.

'No, sir. Nothing,' Sutherland said, politely.

Jones smiled smugly. He took the file handed to him by his assistant, a smart captain in the uniform of a county infantry regiment.

'Thank you, Kingham,' he smiled and then turned to the Head again. 'With your agreement, sir, I wish to raise another matter before I close. This refers to the note I forwarded to you last month, and the minute on file at tab B.'

The Head turned to the marked page in his file and nodded at Jones to continue.

'You are aware of reports concerning German orders for precision instruments placed with French aircraft manufacturers. You'll recall that they obtained some unusual components through these contracts: pressure switches; gyroscopes; and so forth.'

'Yes, I remember the report,' the Head replied.

'Hitherto, our assessment was the Germans were struggling to obtain parts for their bombers. But we can now link this to a secret German project, codenamed *ZINNMAN*.'

'Tin Man? What could that possibly mean?'

'Details, alas, are scanty at this stage, sir. The report emanated from a source within the Grapple network. From a conversation overheard at the Hotel Majestic in Paris and it appears to refer to a special weapon.'

Sutherland knew the Hotel Majestic housed the headquarters of the German administration in occupied France. To have someone within the German central command was a major development, indeed. He sat up in his chair.

'And you believe this lead is valuable enough to justify an uplift in F-Section's budget?'

'Yes,' Jones said, firmly, 'We'll need additional agents, more resources, and greater support from the RAF in transporting people and stores.'

Jones slid a note stamped 'SECRET' down the table.

'This is an estimate of the additional resources required to expand Grapple sufficiently to obtain more details on Tin Man.'

The Head's eyebrows shot up. He removed his spectacles and fixed Jones with a serious look.

'This is not an inconsiderable request, major. If we are to find these resources, it will mean slowing or pausing operations in other areas,' the Head said, gesturing to the country leads for Norway, Denmark, Holland, and Belgium, whose faces wore a range of emotions, none good.

'We believe this *investment*,' he emphasised the word, 'will pay dividends both in expanding our work in northern France and in ensuring that the technological sophistication of the Germans never exceeds our own. If they are developing a wonder weapon, sir, the Prime Minister ought to know about it.'

Sutherland thought it was a cheap shot but admitted it was a crafty move. The S.O.E. was a brainchild of the Prime Minister's, therefore any operation as bold as the one under consideration would likely attract his support. The Head must know this too. With so many other departments competing for funding and attention from the War Cabinet, this proposal had the potential to secure their funding indefinitely. Besides, Grapple was pretty much the only show in town.

'I shall speak with the Director and give you an answer by the end of the week,' the Head replied, after a pause.

The meeting moved onto other topics as each country lead briefed in turn. It eventually wound its way to a natural conclusion until it broke up for lunch. The Head turned to Sutherland, who was packing his documents away into a cardboard box so that they could be destroyed. Looking over his glasses, he appeared not unlike a schoolmaster.

'Colonel Sutherland, may I have a word please?'

The Head's domain was several floors up, away from the frenetic activity and ringing telephones of the staff offices. Sutherland gladly accepted a glass of sherry and admired the room, which was tastefully furnished in dark wood and green leather. *Someone's funding is better than he lets on*, he thought to himself.

'What shall we drink to?'

'Die Hards,' said Sutherland forcefully, drinking it off in one go.

'You were with the 9th Battalion in Baghdad, weren't you?'

'Briefly, in '18.'

'And more recently, I hear?'

Sutherland smiled and replaced the glass on its silver salver.

'I don't think you asked me here for idle chit-chat, sir.'

The Head looked disappointed, but quickly moved on.

'Your question downstairs intrigued me. I got the impression that you have an inside track on our operations,' He said with a sideways glance at Sutherland.

Sutherland said nothing but could not resist the spread of a faint smile.

'Naughty boy, Jumbo. You've been reading our signals,

haven't you? I thought as much, they go through Bletchley after all. So, what impression have you formed of us? Of the S.O.E?'

Sutherland considered the question and picked his words carefully.

'Well, of course you've done an excellent job of creating an organisation like this from the resources you were given. Section D was a fraction of what you have established here-'

'I sense the 'but' coming. Give it to me straight, Sutherland.'

Sutherland glanced at his empty glass, saw that another would not be forthcoming, and sighed inwardly.

'Your overenthusiasm is a weakness,' he said. 'You don't vet your agents thoroughly and, when you do manage to get a network running, your operational security is appalling. Your agents don't compartmentalise, which leaves you vulnerable to exploitation. I think the only reason your existing networks haven't been penetrated to a greater extent is luck, nothing more.'

The Head frowned. He opened his mouth to speak and then closed it again. When he finally did speak, his voice crackled.

'S.O.E. only exists because of failures in *your* organisation. Or have you already forgotten Venlo?'

Sutherland had not forgotten the Gestapo's seizure of British agents at Venlo in 1939 that had so badly damaged continental intelligence gathering. He stiffened at its mention. He had been overseas at the time, but it still smarted.

'You asked for my assessment, sir. That is what you have.'

The Head stared at Sutherland wordlessly for a moment, then he looked away.

'I didn't ask you here to argue about relative merits of our firms. I had a proposition for you. It concerns the Grapple network.'

'I see.'

'It remains a point of fact that F-Section produces some of the best intelligence product for us, at least after the Poles. And this latest development promises to be something of a coup. But I want to be confident that Grapple is all that they say it is. As you said earlier, it would be regrettable if it was proved too good to be true.'

'You don't have confidence in Ivor Jones' claims?'

'It's not that simple. He wants more money, and I find it is always worthwhile checking before trusting. Plus, he's a bloody academic and I can barely tell what he's thinking half the time.'

'Why are you telling me this?'

'I don't possess the means to perform an independent verification of Grapple. But you do. So, I want to offer you a deal – you send someone to verify Grapple and, if it's a scam, then you can crow about it to the rest of the intelligence community.'

Sutherland ran a hand down his face as he considered this. He was still getting used to its smoothness having shaved off his beard after Greece. It meant risking an agent, not a great exchange for the opportunity to rub S.O.E.'s face in it.

'And if Grapple is sound?'

'Obviously, I don't expect something for nothing. I'll share all the Tin Man intelligence with you. But in return I want my own signals intelligence branch – no more using Bletchley. It has to be a *quid pro quo*.'

Sutherland weighed the opportunity in his mind. The right agent would pull off a job like this without trouble. He was excited at the prospect of knowing more about Tin Man, which the Germans had clearly succeeded in keeping secret from his sources on the Continent and from wireless intercepts. His own chief would dislike losing a handle on S.O.E.'s wireless traffic, but it was bound to happen eventually. It was a negligible factor.

'Fine,' Sutherland said. 'I'll need all the details you have on Grapple, the locations of all its safe houses and dead drops, agent details and standard operating procedures.'

'Certainly, I'll ask F-Section to send it over to you this week.'

'I think, to maintain discretion, it would be wise if you asked to review this material personally and then I could arrange for copies to be made for our use. It is only you and I who know about this agreement and we should limit the number of people we share this knowledge with. Don't you agree, sir?'

'Yes, of course.' The Head nodded, but Sutherland detected a slight reluctance. Like he'd not anticipated demands like this. Nevertheless, he shook Sutherland's hand warmly before showing him the door.

Further down the street, Sutherland stepped into a telephone box and picked up the handset. He habitually scanned his immediate surroundings to ensure there was no one within earshot, then he placed a few coins in the slot and dialled the office number. After a couple of rings, the switchboard answered and he pressed the button to talk, hearing his coins drop into the cashbox.

'Put me through to Room 49 please.'

The line clicked and another voice came on the line.

'It's Sutherland here. I need you to find Evelyn Moore.'

Chapter Four

RAF Uxbridge, on the outskirts of London, was the RAF's depot. It was a sprawling estate bursting with people, continually in motion to service the war effort. Here parties of officers and airmen assembled before their drafts overseas, recruits reported for induction into the Service, and the flotsam of unattached, unfit, and unemployed personnel were given new orders or sent to fresh billets.

Charlie hovered in the long, dark sterile corridor in one of the many identical blocks that were scattered about the site. The pain in his temples filled his conscious mind and he rubbed his forehead to attempt to ease it. The attacks had been with him for weeks now, ever since coming around in H.M.S. Alacrity's sick bay, halfway to Gibraltar. He had refused an examination by the Station Medical Officer there, worried that he would be grounded, and instead trusted the pain would recede with time. It came and went now, but when it came it was debilitating.

'Is it the headaches again?'

Charlie jumped at Peter's voice behind him. He realised he was unable to beguile his crewmate, who must have noticed his anguished appearance several times during their stay on the Rock, or on the Sunderland flight back to Plymouth.

'It'll pass, it's just a momentary thing,' Charlie said firmly.

Peter looked doubtful as the door opposite them opened and a firm voice beckoned them in.

A wingless squadron leader sat at a small utilitarian desk in the cramped space. He gestured for them to sit, without looking up from a file on his desk.

'Quite a journey it's been for you both. Egypt, Greece, Gibraltar – wherever next?'

There was a brief silence in which Charlie said inwardly, *that's your job to tell us.*

'Of course,' the Squadron Leader continued, 'It's my job to tell you that. Bit of an odd one this, normally I have to find aircrew to fill squadrons overseas, but this time it's the other way around.' He chuckled to himself.

Charlie let his mind wander away from the awkward, formal encounter to daydream about what he would do with some time off. He wondered whether any of his girlfriends from before the war were at a loose end. It had been quite some time since he'd enjoyed a woman's company. Not since Margot Dacre, he remembered suddenly. He was vaguely aware that the Squadron Leader was addressing him.

'I'm sorry, sir. Did you say something?'

'I asked if you're alright? You look like you're suffering a migraine.' The Squadron Leader spoke slowly and loudly, as if addressing someone who was hard of hearing.

'Quite alright, it's just a passing headache,' Charlie replied.

'I was saying that I don't know where to place the pair of you. If you'd arrived a couple of months ago it would've been night fighters, but the Germans have slacked off lately. Are you hard-over on remaining together?'

'If at all possible, sir,' Peter answered. 'We've been crewed together since Egypt.'

'You have no idea how many don't, you know,' the Squadron Leader shrugged. 'I think it will likely be Bomber Command, but I don't know which squadron yet. It'll take some time to sort something out. Why don't you take a few weeks' leave? I dare say that you'd appreciate it. I'll send you a telegram with details of your new unit before your time is up.'

Charlie had heard the stories about Bomber Command and knew losses had been heavy. Very heavy, in fact. Inadequate aircraft types and the growing strength of Germany's air defences meant the chance of surviving a full tour with Bomber Command was increasingly unlikely. That was fine in his opinion, get it over quickly.

'Perfect,' Charlie said, causing Peter to glance at him.

'Now, to turn to other matters,' the Squadron Leader said, sliding the file away and taking another from a pile on his desk. He flicked it open and drew his finger down the index to find the page he wanted.

'Aha. Here it is. With your time flying anti-shipping patrols on Crete it was under contemplation to put you both in for the Distinguished Flying Cross.'

'That's splendid news, sir,' Peter said, sitting up.

'I said it *was* under contemplation, but unfortunately it didn't quite meet the threshold for recognition, apparently.'

Peter sat back with disappointment etched on his face.

'However, the good news is you've both been promoted to flight lieutenant, so at least you'll receive a modest pay increase.'

Charlie snorted. In his case, the pay rise wouldn't even cover the uniform and belongings he'd lost when they ditched in the Mediterranean. A view he expressed to Peter once they left RAF Uxbridge far behind them.

'You've always got to spoil things, haven't you? This promotion means more than a little more money; it's another step up the ladder,' Peter said.

'It's an empty gesture. "Sorry you didn't get a medal; here's a meaningless promotion", that's what they mean,' Charlie said, placing his hand to his head as a jolt of pain passed through it.

Peter shook his head with obvious exasperation and stopped in the middle of the street.

'I can see why some crews don't want to fly together after a while. There's always someone who drags you down.'

'Oh, that's very nice. How about when I dragged you out of a sinking aeroplane – you weren't moaning then.'

'You always do this.'

'Do what?'

'You take the joy out of it. I know you've been through a hard time, and I'm sorry that it never worked out with Margot, but you've got to move on and start thinking about the future. This promotion means money, and status, and reputation. Don't you want that too?'

Charlie bristled at the mention of Margot Dacre, a Women's Auxiliary Air Force officer he had courted in North Africa and who had dumped him for a soldier when he was in Greece. He didn't think before snapping, 'They say you always crave the most what you possess the least.' He regretted the words the moment they left his mouth.

Peter stared wordlessly at him.

'I'm sorry I-'

'Piss off, Charlie,' Peter said as he walked away.

Charlie watched him go. He felt wretched and his head pounded. He realised he had no idea when he would next see him].

'Fine,' he said to no-one. 'That's just fine.'

*

The high-pitched screech of a train whistle echoed across the platforms, announcing the 20:30 to Bristol was leaving Paddington Station. In the dim canteen Peter sipped the dregs of his tea and tried to ignore the bitter taste of over-stewed leaves. Fifteen minutes to go before the last Plymouth train left. It was the only home he had, and the place he wanted to go least of all. The tea ladies tidied up around him, clinking the mugs to remind him the place shut in half an hour. He lit another cigarette in silent protest and returned to gazing into his cup.

Home. It was a mixed bag for someone with Peter's past. Every memory an unhappy one, every thought was filled with relief at escaping it. Of course, there were other places he could go. Hostels, boarding houses or hotels. There was even a camp near Scarborough that acted as a rest centre for servicemen. But something deep inside told him he needed to face up to his past. To confront it – to be brave.

A gust of cold air on his cheek told him the platform door had been opened a moment before the bell jangled. It brought with it the smelt of soot, steam and oil.

'Hello dear, can I help you?'

He heard one of the tea ladies speak but couldn't make out the reply because he wasn't actively listening. He lost in his thoughts. Small gritty tea leaves pooled in the bottom of his mug. People claimed to be able to tell one's fortune by reading tea leaves. He wondered what this untidy clump said about him.

'Yes, a parachute mine, weeks ago now. It made an awful mess of the station roof,' the lady said in a gossipy tone. Peter glanced up at the wall clock above him, ten minutes to go.

'I'd hoped to find you here, it was the last place I thought to look.'

These words were addressed to him. With a jolt, Peter recognised the voice but could not believe it.

'Eve?'

'Hello, Peter.'

He leapt up, knocking over the cup and twisting about to look at her. Her dark curls emerged from beneath a snuff-coloured beret. A faint smile of amusement creased her face.

'My god, it *is* you. What are you doing here?'

'I read about you in the paper and thought you'd be in London, but when I called Uxbridge they said you'd gone. I tried the Savoy too,' she replied.

'You remembered?'

When Peter had seen Eve last, they agreed to meet again on the day after the war ended. Little did he suspect it would be much sooner than that.

'Of course I did. But where's Charlie?'

Peter made a face and shrugged.

'We quarrelled and I walked off. I think he's gone home to his family. Some place in Wiltshire. I regretted it instantly, but I just couldn't find it in me to be the bigger man.'

'I'm sorry to hear that. And I suppose you're also heading home? I hear that Plymouth took quite a pasting in the bombing. You're probably anxious to see your family too?'

'Not really, it's just my father now and he always seems to come out of scrapes just fine,' Peter said, trying to dismiss a mental image from his youth of his father bruised and beaten after another heavy drinking session.

Eve smiled. Her raincoat was spotted with water and she looked like she wanted to say something but was struggling with the words.

'Will you have a cup of tea, at all?' Peter looked around at the little knot of women who eavesdropped on them from the end of the room. Caught in the act, they pretended to be busy cleaning and he grinned at the sight of the little pantomime.

'No. No, thank you, I mean. I'm sure these girls are keen to shut up and go home for the night.'

Peter searched Eve's face for a clue to the unexpected awkward silence that followed. Should he propose a hotel, he asked himself? It seemed awfully forward, although society was changing quickly during this war. He'd never before seen couples copulating in shop doorways in Bayswater, for example. But then again, before today Peter had never been to Bayswater either. He was flooded with relief when Eve finally spoke, 'Well, if you're not committed elsewhere, I wondered if perhaps you'd like to join me for a few days? I've a little place in the Cotswolds. If we leave now, we might just catch the last train.'

Peter wasn't astonished by Eve's offer. He knew her well enough to understand her disregard for convention. She was a woman who did as she pleased, and she damned anyone who judged her for it. Her independent spirit was one of the reasons why she was so attractive to him.

'I'd be delighted. Thank you,' he said finally.

'Come on then, we'll have to hurry,' she took his hand and led him out of the canteen. As they exited, she turned to him and said, 'But aren't you forgetting something?'

Peter looked back through the windows. His hat was wedged under his left arm and he held his small suitcase in the same hand. He glanced back at Eve in confusion as she stood on her tiptoes and kissed him forcefully, and then gently. He held her in his arms as the shriek of a train whistle announced that the 20:45 to Plymouth was leaving the station.

*

Nyarde Park was a modest Georgian residence sitting at the opening of a chalk valley bordering Cranborne Chase. The estate comprised 112 hectares of grassland and was home to a dairy herd and the village of Frogmell's 67 souls. Whilst Nyarde itself could never have been considered as one of the great country estates of England (it was incomparable to Great Chalfield, or even Lacock for that matter), it shone with shabby charm. Anthony Kendrick, Charlie's father, was proud of this heritage and he rigorously maintained pre-war standards in his home. One of these was dressing for dinner.

Charlie's dinner jacket hung loose about him and the trousers felt baggy. He therefore felt guiltless as he poured out another pre-dinner brandy in the drawing room. On the side table was an telegram posting him to No.44 Operational Training Unit at RAF Abingdon, as an instructor. It was not the frontline, and he'd felt a twinge of disappointment when he read it. He stared out of the window at the grounds just beyond the house and wondered where Peter had been posted.

'You might lay off that occasionally,' Charlie's father said as he entered. 'It's French and I have no idea when we'll be able to get another bottle. Stuff's like hen's teeth.'

He tossed the paper he'd been holding onto the side table. The headline read 'British Sink Bismarck'.

'That's the sort of thing your chaps should be up to,' Anthony Kendrick stated flatly. 'Really handing it to the Hun. Good job we've got the Royal Navy.'

Charlie regarded his father silently. He considered whether there was any point in trying to explain to the old man that the search for and destruction of the German capital ship was a joint operation. It had been a RAF flying boat that sighted Bismarck and permitted naval vessels from Force H to strike her somewhere west of Brest. He pondered how he might explain the intricacies of coordinating air and maritime assets in such a way that they could enable an attack on a moving target in changeable weather in the vast emptiness of the Atlantic Ocean. But he decided it was a hopeless endeavour to a man who had devoted his life to the land and whose interests extended little beyond the management of Nyarde. Instead, he poured a smaller glass for his father, who drank it off and studied his son thoughtfully.

'You look drunk. You're drinking too much.'

'Well what do you expect, there's nothing else to do around here.'

'Nonsense. There's plenty to do. I spend all day doing things. Fences need to be mended or drainage examined, there's never enough time for everything. It's hard to find labour with the war on and you'll need to learn all this before you inherit the Park. The war won't last forever, and I won't live forever either.'

Charlie felt a growing tension behind his forehead, the sign of another of his headaches, even after three glasses of brandy. The drink burned his throat and warmed his belly.

'I can't see me ever running Nyarde. I'm a town mouse. You should sell the land off to the Government or something and retire on the profits. Marjorie's married off now and Flo's with the Women's Voluntary Service, so what do we need all this land for, it's obscene.'

'There's been a Kendrick at Nyarde for four generations,' his father said patiently. 'Quite apart from being saddled with the place, your mother made me promise not to let it go.'

Charlie said nothing. He hadn't expected his mother to feature in this discussion and the mention was momentarily disarming. His father refilled his own glass.

'Before she passed, your mother insisted I followed three rules in bringing you up: you were to go to a good school and then either into medicine or the law; you weren't to marry a tart or a Mitford; and the estate was to go to you, whether you wanted it or not.'

Charlie had barely known his mother, who died shortly after he, the youngest of three children, was born. This was all news to him, and he tried to think of an adequate response. Whilst he was thinking, the dinner gong rang in the hall. His father squeezed his arm.

'Don't make up your mind now, think on it. As you know, Nyarde only came to me because your uncles died in the last war. It would be a shame to let it go before you've worked out what you're going to do after the RAF.'

How can I even think about a life after the war when I can't imagine surviving it in the first place, Charlie thought.

'The responsibility of it all would weigh too heavily on my shoulders,' Charlie replied, 'Nyarde is your life, not mine.'

'Who's to say what life you're going to have? Fate can be a strange mistress.'

Charlie glanced at the telegram on the table. But when he

turned back, he saw his father had already left for dinner.

*

The village of Chearney Down nestled in the rolling hills of the Cotswolds, not far from Chipping Norton. Aside from its small Norman church, a manor farm, parsonage, pub, and post office, it boasted perhaps a dozen dwellings. One of these, a two-bedroom weaver's cottage, was set away from the village green at the edge of a little copse. It was difficult to see from the village, and so the arrival of Peter and Eve went generally unnoticed and unremarked.

Had it been any other way it would not have mattered, because there was no scandal to be found at Bluebell Wood Cottage. Eve made up the spare bedroom for Peter and, to any casual observer, they appeared like brother and sister. They passed the time quite happily together, walking the lanes and backwoods surrounding the village. Eve led Peter to the remains of a Roman villa she had discovered as a child and showed him the mosaic tiles turned up by burrowing creatures.

'You see,' she said holding a few tiles in her palm, 'We think the past is buried away from us. But it's there waiting to be rediscovered and retold.'

He delighted at seeing the passion in her eyes when she spoke about history, which he grudgingly admitted sparked his own interest. She told him about the Romans and the Saxons, and the Normans who followed them. He was enthralled and listened to her with a mixture of fascination and awe.

For his part, Peter cooked. This was one of the few activities Eve did not have a natural talent for. The limit of her culinary skills was cooking an egg. He had learned to fend for himself as a young man and had grown competent at casseroles and stews by helping Mrs Harris next door feed her family. Although wartime made it more difficult to obtain some luxury items, game was plentiful thereabouts and they ate well. There was even a little wine, from dusty bottles retrieved from the garden shed. After dinner they would often sit reading together or gaze at the stars. The summer sky was crisp and clear above Chearney.

These were halcyon days for Peter who only belatedly recognised how badly he needed a rest away from operations. In Eve he had not only his equal, but also a trusted confident. He could tell her about what had happened in Greece, and she listened without judgement. The more he talked, the more the images of burning aircraft and dead men plaguing his dreams faded to the corners of his mind. They never went entirely away, but their presence now rarely affected his mood.

On their walks, Eve opened up to him. She talked about the grief she felt for her father and how she had escaped to Rome, only returning to bury her mother in 1938. She was less candid about her work with Sutherland, choosing to change the subject or only offer vague details when the topic came up. Peter began to understand why she had never needed a man in her life; she had never needed anyone at all.

It was several days before he remembered that he had informed no-one of where to send his posting instructions. He used the telephone in the local post office to call RAF Uxbridge and, after a few attempts, managed to get through to the Squadron Leader. The poor fellow sounded harassed on the phone and was short with Peter.

'Denhay? Yes, I hadn't forgotten about you. In fact, I had your orders prepared at the start of the week when they were changed.'

'Changed, sir? How?'

'I had you going to a nice little operational training unit, heavy bombers at Abingdon. It was a swell deal, but they've been switched by someone at Bomber Command – blast them.'

'Where am I going now?'

'Eh? Oh, it says 1419 Flight, RAF Tangmere. Know anything about them?'

'No.'

'Me neither, old chap. But I'm sure it's suitable and you start a week on Monday. Best of luck with it, cheerio.'

On what was to be their penultimate day at Chearney, although neither knew it, a telegram arrived for Eve. She opened it at the little table next to the kitchen's hearth and her face fell.

'What is it?

'I'm afraid I've had some rather awful news and I need to leave tomorrow.'

Peter sat down.

'When will I see you next?'

'I don't know. Perhaps not for several months-'

The words *perhaps never* died away unsaid.

'This damned war, I hate it,' Peter shook his head.

'This time we've had together has been wonderful,' she said sadly, 'But it had to come to end, otherwise I would want to stay here with you forever. Soon you'll be back flying again, and you won't think of me at all.'

'Don't say that. I think about you all the time,' Peter said. With a deep breath he blurted out, 'I love you.'

Eve laughed at him, covering her mouth to hide her smile, 'You can't love me, you silly boy.'

His cheeks burned with embarrassment.

'Oh, Peter. It's so damned unfair. Just when we've found each other again, to be so cruelly torn apart.'

She leaned forward and kissed him. Then she stood, took Peter's hand, and led him upstairs to her bed.

Chapter Five

The intelligence staff at 11 Northumberland Terrace analysed all the information gleaned from S.O.E. on Grapple and displayed it in the basement's cramped and smoke-filled briefing room. The product covered the walls from waist high to ceiling. In the middle of the room, under a solitary lamp, sat a trestle table holding the equipment that Eve would use for her mission to France. Sutherland spoke slowly and deliberately in his faint Ulster accent as he took her through the brief. He was conscious not to miss anything, nor to focus on anything unduly. It was a testament to his skill as a spymaster that he delivered it entirely from memory.

'You'll be familiar with the cell as the basic unit employed by S.O.E. in France. Each cell comprises a minimum of three members: an organiser, who is the leader; a wireless operator; and a courier. Grapple *also* has an air landings officer and a quartermaster. The former is responsible for choosing landing grounds and arranging supply drops.

'So, five people in total?'

'In the core Grapple network, yes there are only five S.O.E.-trained agents. But, of course, the cell recruits agents locally from the French population to run safe houses or perform surveillance and espionage activity. We don't have the figures for these, but we estimate between 30-40 people.'

Eve frowned, 'That's a big network. No wonder they're worried about penetration.'

Sutherland nodded. Everything he knew about tradecraft told him that it was wise to keep networks small and to subdivide them into autonomous cells. This was called 'compartmentalisation'. Each cell prosecuted its discrete activities with only the intelligence staff in London able to see the big picture across the entire network. This was a security precaution that limited the threat from enemy counter-intelligence by the use of 'cut-outs', trusted intermediaries known to only a handful of people. If a cell was blown, the damage was limited to only those people in the immediate team, rather than the entire network.

'What do you know about the S.O.E. agents – any concerns?'

'The organiser is a chap called Stephen Plainfare – he's one of Ivor Jones' golden boys from Oxford. A subaltern with the Royal Northumberland Fusiliers, he volunteered for S.O.E. in June last year and has been in Paris since February. He's a Type 'A' soldier, if he wasn't doing this he'd be with the Commandos or some other mob like that.'

Sutherland gestured at Plainfare's mugshot. He was a twenty-something, sporting type. Sutherland's first impression was of an arrogant bastard, although he chose not to mention this to Eve.

'Any suspicions about him?'

'Nothing we could dig up. His training scores were good, family are all naturalised for at least a couple of generations,' Sutherland shrugged, moving down the wall.

'Lise Dubreys is his wireless operator. She was recruited from the First Aid Nursing Yeomanry. Mother was French but she grew up in England.'

'A proficient operator?'

'According to her training report, she's no better or worse than the average S.O.E. operator,' Sutherland said, meaning she was pretty dreadful.

'What are her tells?'

'Just sloppy, rushed procedures really. Her training report warned that her use of security checks was intermittent. You'll understand that the security checks are a series of characters transmitted at the front and back of a signal that confirm an agent isn't operating under duress.'

'What does S.O.E. think about that?'

'Difficult to tell. Wireless operators are often under pressure to get a message away; it's not unusual for them to slip up.'

Eve looked dissatisfied for the first time since the brief started, Sutherland recalled that her own wireless telegraphy was flawless.

'She's also related to the network's air landing officer, Andre Dubreys,' Sutherland said, pointing to another photo.

'Her husband?'

'Brother. He's a former French army officer. Came over after Dunkirk and went back shortly after with RF-Section in Marseilles. But, apparently, he's not fond of De Gaulle.'

Sutherland hinted at the complicated nature of resistance in occupied France, which S.O.E. divided into different sections according to their tribal loyalties or political persuasions. RF-Section was pro-Gaullist, but F-Section was not.

He went in recently, I see,' Eve said, studying a post-sortie report filed by the RAF.

'Yes. The RAF brought him back for training after they almost lost an aircraft near Chartres.'

'I recognise him, we were on the same parachuting course together.'

Sutherland paused to consider this unexpected news. If Dubreys was a rat, then this might expose Eve to unnecessary danger. But if she did not travel courtesy of Dubreys' landing services, Eve could pick and choose the time of their meeting.

'Would he recognise you?'

'Possibly not, there were many of us on the course.'

'It'll have to be a blind drop then. Does that worry you?'

Sutherland knew the answer before he'd even asked the question.

'No, just tell the RAF not to fly too low.'

'Sure, it'll be like descending on the moving staircase at The Angel,' Sutherland smiled.

'What about the Quartermaster?'

'Victor Resonet is French Canadian. Strictly speaking he doesn't belong to Grapple at all, he supports all F-Section operations and operates through a cut-out. He's the one I trust most of all. If Grapple is a hoax, he's the person least likely to have been compromised and I would recommend you contact him early on.'

Resonet looked like a typical intelligence agent to Sutherland, in that he was instantly forgettable. Sparse, short hair above a round, featureless face and small dark eyes. You wouldn't pick him out of a crowd; he would be a nightmare to track down.

'Finally,' Sutherland continued, 'the courier, Yvette Gallois. She's the youngest of the lot at 21, came across with her husband who was killed flying for the RAF last summer. She volunteered for S.O.E. shortly after that.'

'Do you think she's out for revenge?'

'We hope so, although her file is less convincing. She scored badly on her assessments and wasn't recommended for operations.'

'So how did she end up in France?'

'Necessity, I suspect. S.O.E. is desperate for agents and it looks like standards have been lowered,' Sutherland replied. There were several explanations for overriding the recommendation of S.O.E.'s training officer, including the possibility that Gallois just didn't fit the mould. For an unconventional organisation, the training and selection of agents was a depressingly conventional process.

Sutherland led Eve towards the table saying, 'Your mission is to determine, beyond doubt, whether Grapple remains secure. Nothing else, and no heroics.' Sutherland sounded unnaturally firm, even for an Ulsterman.

'Understood,' Eve said with a smile. It left him wondering whether he was softening with age. Eve knew the risks she was taking; she knew the drill. Nevertheless, he decided not to tell her that he had taken some precautions to ensure her safety. Only a week ago he'd exerted some pressure to get Bomber Command to post Peter Denhay to the RAF's Special Duties unit. He was aware that they were in a relationship, and the man was clearly competent at the role from his time in Greece. It helped having someone on the inside, even if the fellow didn't know it yet.

'Here is a list of all our safe houses. You'll need to memorise it. This pack contains details of your escape line; the same applies. This is a Grapple line, not one of MI9's, so the utmost caution is advised. Only use this route if you have no other options.'

He unfolded a map on the table, which showed northern France in detail.

'Your dropping ground is between Paris and Dreux, on the edge of this large forest. It should give you plenty of options to make your way to Paris. Here's money and identity cards for your use, your ration card and travel papers - all forged, of course. Your identity details are here, you're a widow looking for work. Clothing with the maker's marks removed, it's all in the French style, and your side arm. A Colt .32 automatic.'

'I've used one before,' Eve said, handling the snub-nosed pistol.

'Now, your coat,' Sutherland handed her a thick woollen overcoat, it was an ugly dun-coloured thing with a belt that looped about the middle, 'Twist the second button from the top to release its lid, you'll find a cyanide ampule within. Bite down on it to break the glass and release the poison. It should take effect within minutes.'

'That's a relief,' Eve replied.

'It goes without saying that you must not fall into enemy hands,' Sutherland repeated.

'I was expecting a radio, I can hardly call London from a telephone.'

'We have a dead drop location in Paris, the details are in your pack. You'll find a wireless set there. But Lise Dubreys should be a priority for you too.'

Eve said nothing but glanced about the room at all the photos and papers that were pinned to the walls. He could tell that she was troubled, almost as if he could read her mind. She was like a daughter to him really, he reflected, even though he'd never had time for children.

'This should be entirely straightforward for you,' he said finally, 'You've had tougher assignments. I'll expect regular contact.'

'If anything goes wrong, Jumbo-'

'It won't.'

'-But if it does. Promise me you won't send anyone after me. If it goes wrong, then you mustn't sacrifice someone else.'

Sutherland studied her face, recognising the mute, desperate appeal in her eyes. It was unnerving. He considered Evelyn Moore to be an exceptional agent and rock solid to boot, but this was a new side to her.

'I promise I'll not send anyone after you if it goes wrong,' Sutherland replied. The lie rolled off his lips with a smoothness that came with years of practice.

*

In the gloomy half-light of the aerodrome, the Whitley bomber stood out like a caricature of an aeroplane. A pencil with wings, Eve thought. But what wings. Big, rectangular lifting surfaces - no wonder it was nicknamed 'The Flying Barn Door' by its crews.

Dressed in her issued unmarked clothing, she donned a heavyweight green jumping suit and strapped a parachute harness over that. Her other equipment was packed into a separate canvas bag by a soldier from the Royal Army Service Corps, it would be dropped by separate parachute. The final items she equipped herself with were a padded cloth helmet and her pistol. She tucked this into a pocket on the jumping suit, after checking the magazine was full. In this get-up, she joked, she looked just like the Michelin Man.

Sutherland was quiet and pale; she wished he hadn't insisted on escorting her to the airfield. She had enough on her mind without worrying about his mood too. He stood silently next to her, toying with the buttons on his khaki tunic. Next to the aircraft was a little knot of aircrew who were busy briefing prior to the sortie. The Dispatcher detached himself from the group and, flinging the dregs of his tea into the grass, strolled over to her.

'Evening love, first flight is it?'

'No. Is it yours?

The Dispatcher looked momentarily surprised and then burst out laughing.

'You're a saucy one. I'll check your equipment and run you through the dropping brief now,' he replied.

'I'm all ears.'

He scanned over Eve's rig with an electric torch, searching for the sort of mistakes that nervous agents made (straps not tightened, buckles not done up). Finding none, he nodded with satisfaction and spoke in a practiced tone.

'After take-off just make yourself comfortable, it's quite cramped but the flight time is only an hour and a half. About five minutes before the drop, we'll douse the cabin lights and I'll hook up your static line. I'll show you it, so you know it's connected. Just give me a thumbs up to tell me you're ready.

Then I'll open the floor hatch and ask you to sit on the edge, facing forwards. When I tap your arm, you go. Any questions?'

'No.'

'Fine, I'll give you a moment to say goodbye and then it's "all aboard the Skylark". Do you need airsickness tablets?'

Eve shook her head.

The RAF man walked off still chuckling to himself and Sutherland offered her his hip flask. She took a gulp and felt the strong, antiseptic taste. Scotch, as always. She made a face.

'I'll bring you some champagne back.'

'See that you do. Keep your wits about you.'

'I bet you say that to all the girls,' Eve winked. 'Well, goodbye, Jumbo. Listen out for me.' She did not look back as she walked towards the aircraft, pulling the helmet on as she went. The Dispatcher helped her up into the fuselage and within minutes they were climbing into the night sky.

Eve sat in the cramped space with her knees drawn up, her senses dulled by the roar of the engines. She was feeling nauseous and tasted copper in her mouth, which she thought was oncoming airsickness. She cursed her decision to decline airsickness tablets because they caused drowsiness. A sudden weariness overcame her and soon she dozed happily, her chin resting on the parachute bag. She dreamed of Chearney Down, and Peter, and an airfield in Greece where they met for the first time.

A gentle shove brought her round to a world bathed in red light. The Dispatcher pointed to his watch and held up his hand with all fingers outstretched: five minutes. He clipped on her static line, pulling at it theatrically to show it was firmly attached. Eve gave a thumbs-up and shuffled forward to the hatch, her heart in her mouth. She felt the rush of cold air on her face as the dropping hatch was opened. The roar of the engines diminished; the moment approached. Her feet dangled in the void.

A look downwards revealed a deep impenetrable darkness, she was jumping into the abyss. The Dispatcher stared forwards, away from her, at the red jumping light. She wanted this trial to be over now and closed her eyes to steal herself for the inevitable. There was the tap on her shoulder. She crossed her arms and dropped.

The sensation of falling caused her momentary panic, but she forced herself to straighten her body as she fell. She was pulled up by a violent jerk and then heard the aeroplane droning away into the starry night. The crack of silk pulled tight told her the canopy had filled and several hundred yards away but higher up, her equipment bag floating down lazily. She held the risers and looked about, her eyes adjusting quickly to the dark.

The ground rushed up. The dark mass of a forest stood some way off and immediately below was a pasture. With legs bent and body braced for impact, she landed feet first and rolled over onto her side to absorb the force of the landing. She lay there for a moment, winded, feeling the canopy tugging insistently at her harness as it was plucked by the gentle breeze. Then she slid onto her belly and crawled down the risers to collapse it. *Not a bad start*, she told herself.

Canopy gathered about her like a fur, she clambered over a stone wall and jogged towards the forest where her accompanying load dangling from a tree. There was a collapsible shovel in the bag and she was digging a shallow ditch for her parachute equipment, just inside the forest, when she heard the unmistakable sound of a twig cracking. The pistol was out of its pouch in an instant and she crouched to make herself the smallest possible target. Her heart thumped such that she felt it in her temples and cold sweat tickled down the small of her back. The pistol felt suddenly slippery in her hand; she gripped it harder.

Open-mouthed, she strained to listen for movement in the forest, imagining the approach of a silent hunting group, expecting the bark of dogs in the night, the beam of an electric torch or a shot. The wind carried through the trees gently, nothing more. She relaxed, stood up and caught sight of a figure for the first time. Momentary shock, then relief as she recognised a doe, 20 yards away, staring back at her in surprise. It sniffed the air then turned tail and careened away into the depth of the forest. Eve laughed quietly and wondered who should be more scared on a night like this.

Chapter Six

Charlie's new C.O. inspected him with a dissatisfied look in the cramped hangar office at RAF Abingdon. Rain was falling and a low cloud base meant that flying was off. Nevertheless, the engineers had rolled out a few of the unit's Whitleys for form's sake and Charlie could see their blurred forms through the window behind Squadron Leader Chappell's head.

Chappell. The C.O. pronounced it 'Kapell' in his nasally accent, but Charlie had asked for 'Chapel' when he presented himself and the reaction of instantaneous dislike was visible. Charlie sighed inwardly.

'Have you been drinking, Flight Lieutenant Kendrick?' Chappell sniffed the air, giving an even greater impression of a curious weasel than ever before.

'I had a glass of sherry with lunch, sir,' Charlie said. It was not a lie; he *had* consumed a sherry at lunch. But he saw no reason to admit he had also drunk two pints of ale at the train station, followed by several more swigs of his father's brandy, surreptitiously decanted into his hip flask that morning. The drink helped. It didn't stop the headaches, it just made them more bearable.

'Well, I suppose I ought to welcome you to No.44 Operational Training Unit,' Chappell said. 'Although you're late reporting. We expected you on Monday.'

'I gather there was some confusion with the telegram, sir. My orders clearly stated 10th June,' Charlie replied, waving the orders confidently.

'Regardless, I can't abide lateness. I run this unit like a tight ship. I can describe my command philosophy in three words: discipline, discipline, and discipline. Our mission is to turn out trained aircrews for Bomber Command, ready for the frontline. So, we must be a well-oiled machine – I'll have no squeaky wheels on my training staff. Are you a squeaky wheel, Kendrick?'

'No sir. I'm well oiled.' Charlie suppressed a smile. Chappell paused suspiciously before continuing.

'The demand for aircrew is high. Losses in Bomber Command have been – substantial,' Chappell wrestled with the word. 'Consequently, we are obliged to do everything to ensure trainees pass smoothly through our hands. When we meet our training targets, I look good and you look good. Do you take my meaning?'

'I think so, sir. You expect us to do our best to ensure they make the standard?'

'Including reinterpreting the standard where necessary,' Chappell added, passing over it quickly. Charlie considered this for a moment. It didn't seem right. If crews could not pass muster at the operational training unit, then logic dictated they would be a danger on operations. Therefore, they must be cut from training. To lower the training standard was to pass on the risk to frontline squadrons where the risks were already very high, from what he'd heard. He shifted uneasily in his seat.

'Well, the standard isn't negotiable. That's what the word "standard" means. It's a question of men's lives.'

Chappell laughed humourlessly. Taking a cigarette case from his tunic, he lit one and returned the case to his pocket without offering it to Charlie. He took a long drag and exhaled across the desk.

'You'll see what I mean when you start. It's never so black and white. Being an instructor is a privilege. Most of the others had to complete 30 operations to be selected for this-'

'I've flown *more* than 30 operations on Blenheims in Egypt and Greece.' Charlie tried to maintain a neutral tone, but his temper flared up at the implication he had not earned this appointment. He decided not to mention that he'd been shot down on one of those operations, only surviving by skill and luck. Chappell's own tunic was free of medal ribbons, Charlie noticed.

'Just toe the line, Kendrick,' Chappell said, pushing his chair back to signal their discussion was over.

'I wouldn't dream of doing anything else, sir. I did mean to ask you, however, whether Flight Lieutenant Denhay has reported too? I'd like to continue flying with him if possible.'

'Denhay? Never heard of him.'

*

Although RAF Tangmere was an operational station, it was quieter today than it had been a year before. Situated near Chichester on the south coast, at the height of the Battle of Britain it had been firmly on the frontline. Its fighter squadrons saw daily action against swarms of Luftwaffe fighters and bombers, and the station itself still sported the scars of heavy bombing. Now, the resident fighter unit, the Bader Wing, was dispersed across two other satellite airfields nearby. It only made its presence felt when forming up over the coast prior to another Circus operation, somewhere in northern France.

With the excitement he felt at joining a new squadron, Peter barely noticed the occasional derelict building or emergency repairs made to the hangars. Officially, Peter's unit was a flight and not a squadron. Unusually for the RAF, nobody to whom he'd spoken had a clue about its role or purpose. His driver dropped him outside the single-story brick building that served as its headquarters. It was stranded on a lonely dispersal, well away from the main camp. He counted three Lysanders parked on concrete pads some way off from the building. At least, he thought they were Lysanders. The outline was familiar, but these were painted matt black from undercarriage to wing-root.

Perhaps there was an important brief on elsewhere, he thought to himself; the whole site was like a ghost town.

The familiar smell of cigarette smoke and floor polish met him as he entered the building. Somewhere down the hall a jazz record played. He recognised the tune in a flash, a catchy little Cab Calloway number entitled *The Jumpin' Jive*. It brought a smile to his face and he was just whistling the opening bars of the chorus when he turned the corner into the main hallway and ran straight into a squadron leader holding a teacup.

'Oi!' The Squadron Leader brushed tea off his uniform and looked irritated.

'I'm so sorry, sir, I didn't see you there.'

'Quite,' The Squadron Leader replied with a smile. 'Can I help?'

'Denhay, sir. I'm posted in.'

'Are you indeed? Well I'm Cahill, Archie Cahill. I'm the boss. But don't call me "sir", nobody uses ranks around here,' Cahill rebuked him gently. He withdrew into a cramped office across the corridor and beckoned to Peter. Through the window behind Cahill's head, some engineers were wondering out to one of the Lysanders in an untidy gaggle.

'I wasn't expecting you, to be honest. I had my eyes on another pilot. We're quite a close-knit group, you see. What's your flying experience?'

'I flew Blenheims in the Mediterranean.'

'North Africa?'

'Yes sir-'

'Archie.'

'Yes, Archie. And Greece.'

'That was a hard luck job, how many hours have you got?'

'Just over 400 hours, sir. Archie.'

'How many at night?'

'Oh, hardly any.'

Cahill whistled quietly to himself and looked thoughtful.

'We usually insist on a minimum of 250 night hours, but most of the chaps have double that. Every little helps when you're a pick-up pilot.'

'A pick-up pilot? Is that what you do?'

'Goodness me, didn't you *volunteer* for Special Duties? Our job is to fly into enemy territory by night to drop off or collect friendly agents engaged in espionage. Our pilots fly by moonlight to land on rough airstrips illuminated by electric torches. Ever done anything like that?'

Peter thought for a moment. He had a suspicion that this was no coincidence.

'I've landed a Blenheim in a field that was 250 yards long with a cross-wind.'

Cahill laughed, 'You never? Well, it's something I suppose. You'll have to tell me more about that later, it sounds exactly like something you'd read in a Line Book.'

Peter felt like Cahill was studying him with curiosity. It was only at this point he realised Cahill wore the purple and white ribbon of the Distinguished Flying Cross, or D.F.C., on his tunic. He made a mental note to ask him about this later. Cahill leaned back and placed his hands behind his head.

'I don't normally make exceptions, but you seem like a nice enough chap. We'll have to tailor a training programme for you, but nothing's impossible with a bit of ginger. Now, come and meet the others.'

Walking down the corridor towards the music, Cahill explained to him how 1419 Flight worked. It was nominally based at RAF Newmarket, but used Tangmere as a forward operating base to extend the range of the aircraft deeper into occupied Europe. Moonlight was an essential ingredient in Special Duties flying because it allowed a pilot to navigate at low-level by night. This meant that operations always took place a week either side of a full moon.

The pilot's rest room was a cluttered, untidy space with a stove in one corner and a collection of battered leather armchairs strewn about haphazardly. Peter thought it had 'character', like the men who inhabited it. Slim McKenna was a lively Scot who had spent all his wartime service in Bomber Command. His was the jazz music playing on the gramophone. A giant with a booming voice and a dry, northern wit unfurled himself from one corner and introduced himself as Roger Parsloe. He crushed Peter's hand with a chuckle and told him that flying Special Duties operations would improve his handicap. Colin Webb, however, looked about Peter's age with unruly dark hair and freckles. He was a quiet, unassuming young man who wore a public-school scarf inside his open collar.

'Colin,' Cahill said, 'take Peter out and show him around a Lizzie, will you?'

'Righto, Archie,' Colin replied.

As they walked out to the dispersal, Colin said, 'Lizzie's our pet name for the Lysander. She had a hard time in France doing daylight army cooperation missions with the Krauts hanging about, but she's just perfect for what we need her to do.'

'And what's that?'

'Dumping her in farmers' fields, mostly. Sling out the Joes, that's what we call the agents you understand? Collect another bunch and make a run for it. I'd take this over bombing the Ruhr any day.'

Up close, Peter could see how different these specially modified Mark III aircraft were to the other types in RAF use. Aside from the paint scheme, it carried a 150-gallon external fuel tank between the undercarriage legs. This extended the range of the aircraft to about 1,000 miles. Colin showed him the sliding rear canopy and boarding ladder that had been attached to encourage a swift passenger transfer.

'You can take a couple of Joes in the back in comfort, or a few more in discomfort. D'you know the Boss, Archie, brought out four on one job,' Colin said with pride. 'Almost ran out of juice on the way back and landed in thick fog at Manston.'

'Is that what he got the D.F.C. for?'

'What? God knows, he never talks about it. Why don't you jump up and I'll talk you through the controls?'

Peter clambered up the leg strut to the high cockpit and, throwing his leg over into the open window, gained his seat. Colin appeared next to him and leant in through the open window. Peter surveyed the view from pilot's seat.

'I'm surprised what a great view you have from up here.'

'She was built with that in mind. I think you're familiar with the Bristol Mercury engine, so I won't bore you with engine controls. I do need to explain a few foibles though.'

'Fire away.'

'First there's the automatic flaps and slats. They're designed to function when the aircraft reaches stalling speed in the correct attitude-'

'So, no flap lever?'

'No. Or hydraulics for that matter. The aircraft does it all for you, but you need to be careful – for example, if you find yourself too low on approach and then push the nose forward, the flaps will retract.'

Peter said nothing; that was some drawback.

'It also means you don't let the nose drop on take-off. You just hold it in a nose-high altitude and she just sort of pops off the ground. You'll be surprised how short the take-off roll is.' Colin smiled, he looked less bashful when he was talking about the aeroplane. It was clearly a subject he was passionate about.

'Then there's the brakes,' Colin continued, 'The undercarriage is really strong, it has to be, but the brakes fade fast. You can usually stop in less than 300 yards with only a little application of braking. But bear in mind if you get brake fade then turning the aircraft on the ground is next to impossible.'

'You've experienced that?'

'Not me personally. Slim told me about it, he's got some real stories to make your hair stand on end. Now, finally, trimming. Lizzie is a very stable aircraft in flight, but she hates being out of trim for landing and take-off. You have to be rigorous about checking where your trim is set because if you demand power and trim simultaneously, you might find yourself unable to move the controls. I can't tell you what a bad day that would be.'

'Have you always been on Lizzies then?'

'Oh no,' Colin grinned. 'I was on Hurricanes last year and only came over in January.'

'Hurricanes? You flew in the Battle of Britain?'

'A little, towards the end. I was with 229 Squadron at Northolt.'

'I bet that was hairy?'

'It could be at times, yes. In fact, I wrote a poem about it. Want to hear?'

Peter paused for a moment longer than was polite, before saying, 'Sure, why not?'

Colin cleared his throat, steadied his breathing and, in a voice calculated for the theatre he intoned,

'The sky it burned in violent fight;
We watched them from the 'field;
As aircraft fell, flaming bright;
They gave but did not yield.'

Peter stared dumbly at Colin as the latter coughed to indicate he was finished.

'Well, what do you think?'

'Oh, gosh. It's like nothing else I've heard,' Peter said finally, which was the truth. He believed it was the kindest thing to say under the circumstances.

'It's just something that came to me one day, in between sorties,' Colin shrugged. His cheeks reddened.

'Do you write often?'

'Whenever I get the chance. Would you like to hear something about a burnt-out Heinkel I saw once?'

'Oh, perhaps later. Did you have much night experience on fighters?'

'A little, mostly when Jerry was bombing London by night. My dead-reckoning improved after that.'

'In my last squadron I had someone to do all that for me,' Peter said, suddenly remembering Charlie and their angry exchange at Uxbridge. He regretted it enormously, for many reasons.

'I wouldn't be gloomy about it. You'll pick it up quickly. Before long it'll be totally normal to fly the aircraft with one hand, hold your map in the other, and look out for references at the same time. That's why we fly by moonlight.'

'Because it favours the attacker?'

'Why else would they call it "A Bomber's Moon"?'

*

It was a half moon, rather than a Bomber's Moon, that Charlie spied through the small porthole in his Whitley's fuselage. He glanced at his watch again and swore. They had missed the turning point, as he knew they would. He knew it because this crew was cursed with a truly awful navigator and seemed unable to help him out by working as a team. Consequently, they were also failing as a crew. The Skipper could have given him a nudge or two, at least hinted that the large body of water beneath them was probably the Bristol Channel, but he didn't bother.

This was the fifth practice bombing sortie he'd flown with this crew and, if he had his way, it would be the last. Chappell was deaf to his appeals, however. He'd recommended in the strongest possible terms that the crew be split up. Obviously, something was not working for this particular set of men. It happened occasionally. He knew as much as anyone else how important crew cohesion was. It was literally a matter of life or death when a rear-gunner's call was all they had to alert them to a night fighter creeping up on them out of the gloom. He made up his mind to fail them. Be damned to Chappell's figures, the sodding bureaucrat.

Flying Officer Semple, the trainee navigator, stared blankly at the chart in front of him, ignoring the minute hand of his stopwatch ticking away the time since the course correction they had not made, and never would now.

'Where do you think you are?'

Semple turned to him, his face filled with the misery of self-evident failure. He pointed his pencil with little certainty to a spot just above Gloucester.

'No,' Charlie said. 'You're about 50 miles south-west of there and heading towards Lundy. It doesn't sound much, but it could be the difference between missing a flak concentration and flying straight through it.'

'I did all the calculations like I was supposed to,' Semple said. 'Perhaps I got the wind speed wrong?'

'Look, Semple, there's no shame in calling it quits, you know. It could be that navigation's not for you. There are plenty of other ways to fight this war.'

'But all I ever wanted to do was fly-' Semple's words died on his lips, his eyes filled instead. Charlie looked away in the knowledge he hadn't the heart to fail a crying man. With his back turned he handed off instructions to Semple.

'Tell the Skipper to put us back on a course of 084 degrees, then work out the time from Bristol to Abingdon. That should get you into the overhead. And for Christ's sake don't forget to tell him to descend below 5,000 feet on the way back, otherwise we'll meet the operational traffic coming the other way.'

Charlie pulled the curtain back across the navigator's station and fumbled around for his bag. Checking that the eyes of the crew were elsewhere, he untwisted the top of his hipflask and took a deep draught. His head pounded as it always did when he was under strain and he wondered again whether he should report it to a doctor. If he did, he would certainly be grounded, perhaps indefinitely, and he had no desire to see the war out shining his arse in some office job when other men were doing the fighting.

The flask sounded dry. He shook and then upended it; it *was* dry. He sensed the beginnings of an unreasonable mood. He had only topped the thing up that morning with cheap Scotch from a bottle a previous occupant had left in his mess room. And he had not felt the aircraft begin its descent yet.

He briefly entertained the idea of reminding Semple himself, but then decided he could not face the man's sordid tears. He'd tell the pilot himself and, sliding around the navigator's station he climbed up to the cramped cockpit. The Skipper flashed him a smile from his seat. It was a look that said *I might have an idiot for a navigator but at least I can land this damned thing.*

Lit by the faint red glow of the instruments, the cockpit was only marginally brighter than the surrounding sky. The whole country was still under the blackout imposed in 1939. A thin wisp of cloud hung beneath them, reflecting the moonlight, but otherwise they might have been flying over a vast ocean of darkness. It still impressed him to see it from the air.

He plugged his headset lead into the intercom and was about to speak when he caught sight of a deeper blackness emerging from the corner of his vision. No more than a fraction of a second passed before he screamed to the pilot, 'Break left, now!'

The Whitley dropped into a sharp dive and then the port wing dipped, throwing Charlie over the pilot's seat. He struggled to pull away from the pilot who was himself fighting to recover the bomber from the emergency manoeuvre. Straining his neck to look upwards, Charlie glimpsed the unmistakable shadow of another large aircraft swoop over them. It was so close he could see the blue exhaust flames as it passed overhead, apparently oblivious to the mid-air collision it had avoided.

'Sorry about that everyone,' the Skipper said when he levelled off at 1,000 feet. 'I had to avoid another aircraft. All ok?'

The crew reported in from their various positions, the gunners, wireless operator, and Semple – all ok. Charlie was not ok, however. Cold sweat ran down his back and his head felt like someone was tightening a belt around it. He'd told Semple to pass the order to descend, but Semple had not followed this basic instruction. Fuming with rage, Charlie left the cockpit and snatched back the curtain, causing Semple to jump in surprise.

'Why didn't you pass the order to descend onto the Skipper? You nearly killed us back there.'

'I forgot. I was trying to plan the route back to base. I'm sorry.'

'Stick "I'm sorry" up your pipe. You're chopped. Now bugger off and let me at the chart table.

The Whitley bounced down the flare path at Abingdon. It taxied off the field to the apron beside the large hangars, where the pilot shut down. Charlie had nothing further to say to Semple, or anyone else, and lowered himself from the fuselage onto firm ground. It was only a short march to the Officers'

Mess, which he entered in full flying gear and went straight to the bar. It was after supper and there was a reasonably large crowd. At the sight of him, a gap appeared at the bar, which he filled immediately. He was thankful that everyone could recognise a man in a funk and knew to leave him alone.

'Give me a double Scotch and soda. Please,' Charlie said to the mess steward. Adding, a heartbeat later, 'On second thoughts, don't bother with the soda.'

Charlie sent the Scotch down in a swift gulp, thumping the glass down onto the bar.

'Another.'

It duly arrived and was dispatched with the same ferocity. Burning down to his stomach, it brought an instant relief to his fragile nerves, but not the ghastly pain that radiated from his temples. The request for a third was yet unborn in his throat when Chappell's nasally voice met his ears.

'I say. I say, Kendrick. You know the rules about flying clothing in the mess. I'm going to have to ask you to leave.'

'I'll leave when I'm ready,' Charlie grunted, signalling again to the steward. 'And, I ain't ready.'

The conversation around them died away as the other drinkers picked up on what was likely to be an ugly spat.

'I beg your pardon?' Chappell glanced to his left and right, clearly flabbergasted at this public affront.

'And I'll tell you another thing. Chappell,' he pronounced it 'Chapel'. 'I'm washing out that bloody crew you've given me. They're all wrong; they'll get themselves killed. They nearly killed *me* tonight.'

Chappell leaned in close to Charlie and hissed at him, 'You drunken sot. Do you think you can talk to me like that? I'll break you. I'll-'

'Oh, shove it.' Charlie turned back to the bar, leaving Chappell open-mouthed.

'Don't you turn your back on me,' Chappell replied. Charlie felt Chappell's hand grasp his shoulder, pulling him away from his drink. It enraged him.

'Get your damned hands off me,' Charlie growled. It was a warning, but Chappell persisted. Everyone's attention was drawn to the unseemly tussle between the two men. The silence was deafening. Charlie tried once more to shake off Chappell's grip, failed, and swung a fist in a desperate bid for freedom. It was not a great punch, it lacked both power and firmness, but it landed squarely on Chappell's nose and dropped him immediately. He sprawled on the floor in an untidy clump.

'I told you to leave me alone,' Charlie said, rubbing his knuckles.

Chappell looked up in shock at the blood on his hand.

'You broke my nose, you bastard. Someone call the RAF Police. I'll have you for this Kendrick. You're finished.'

Charlie guessed it would take the RAF Police five minutes or so to arrive. He reached out for his glass once more; deciding it might be his last for a while.

Chapter Seven

Peter stared idly out of the window of his barren mess room as the light of another summer's day receded. An insistent Blue Tit outside shrilled its distinctive song, which brought a smile to his face. Soon he would pull on his flying boots, smoke a last cigarette, and head over to the dispersal for his first operational mission as a pick-up pilot. A thorough introvert, he enjoyed solitude because the quiet and calmness felt good for his soul. The previous weeks had been like nothing else he had ever encountered, practicing low-level navigation by night and flying into a temporary airstrip set up for him in the New Forest.

He proved to be a natural and was soon given a mission to fly to a point in central France and report what he'd seen there. Peter located it after a nerve-wracking flight of three hours, a bright point of light shining in a sea of blackness. Astounded, he'd marked his map and turned for home, taking care not to fly too close to the illuminated feature. When he reported it to Archie on his return to Tangmere, the Squadron Leader shook his hand heartily and welcomed him to 1419 Flight. It had been a final test, and Peter had passed.

To celebrate his initiation to the Flight, the other pilots staged a party at Tangmere Cottage, a requisitioned building just outside the base. They had opened several bottles of champagne, which had been smuggled out of France, and invited some girls from the station. Slim played his jazz music loud. There was, of course, singing and dancing. Roger performed a party trick he called 'The French Horn' where he broke wind to the opening bars of La Marseillaise. Colin proved to be a hit with the women, at least until he recited his poetry, but was last seen disappearing into the bushes at the back of the property with one of the clerks from the General Office.

It had been a fabulous evening. A rare night of celebration in what felt like, to Peter, a long bloody war. Of course, he felt guilty at having such a good time when Eve was God knows where. Even worse, with all the flying, he hadn't bothered to call Charlie to find out how he was doing. This was unpardonable because they had parted with angry words. He checked his watch, there was still time.

In the lobby, Peter scanned the telephone directory until he found the entry for the appointing office at RAF Uxbridge, then asked the operator to call the numbers from top to bottom in order until each in turn rang out. The very last one picked up and an irritated duty clerk answered. Peter asked for Charlie's details and the clerk told him to wait a moment while he searched his register. Peter checked his watch, his car would arrive in the next five minutes. The clerk returned, checked Charlie's service number and gave Peter the details for No.44 Operational Training Unit at RAF Abingdon. Peter called the operator back and asked to be put through to the Duty Flying Supervisor. This time the call was answered almost immediately.

'Good Evening, Flying Supervisor speaking.'

'Oh hello, I don't suppose Flight Lieutenant Kendrick is flying tonight please?'

'Kendrick? You're about a day late, chum. Kendrick's been chopped off the squadron, I think he's awaiting court-martial.'

'Court-martial?' Peter replied with surprise, 'For what?'

'He punched the Boss.'

'That can't be right.'

'I can't agree more, he deserves a bloody medal.'

'Where is he now?'

'He's under arrest. Look, I can't stand around here gossiping all night, I've a job to do.'

The phone went dead. Peter heard his car pull up outside, it sat there with the engine ticking over. He was at a complete loss for words. Charlie must be in a very bad place indeed if he really had thumped a senior officer. He was out of time but grabbed a nearby pad of paper and scribbled furiously. He tucked the note into his flying jacket and jumped into the car.

At the dispersal, he ran over the flight plan with Colin who was on duty that evening. The mission had been telephoned through from S.O.E. earlier that day. The sortie folder was marked 'GRAPPLE IX'. It proved to be a single agent drop-off with accompanying freight, most likely arms and communication equipment. The landing ground selected was a disused aerodrome near Amiens. It was not a difficult run, a channel crossing to cut the French coast near Le Tréport, then pick up the course of the Somme roughly south-east, skirting south about Amiens where the lights of the landing ground should be seen.

'There's a 50 percent chance of low-lying fog forming overnight in coastal areas,' Colin said, gesturing to the meteorological report.

'Should I worry about that?'

'You can always climb above it. If you can't get back in to Tangmere then you should divert to Manston or Odiham.'

'Righto.'

'The Joe's here. You want to chat to him before you walk?'

'Sure,' Peter said.

A young man in an ill-fitting suit poked his head around the door. Peter waved him over as he emptied his own pockets into a wooden box proffered by Colin. He found the note he had scribbled in his flying jacket and pressed it into Colin's hand.

'I've some unfinished business that needs to be done tonight. Do you mind?'

'Not at all, how can I help?'

'Can you track down a fellow called Johnny Corbett, he's a squadron leader or a wing commander, maybe. When you do, read him that and tell him it's from me.'

'Cripes, don't you have enough cloak and dagger in your life?'

'You'll do it, Colin?'

'Leave it with me,' Colin smiled. Peter knew he could trust him.

The Joe coughed, he stood awkwardly at the table as if he was a mere afterthought rather than the purpose of tonight's mission. Archie had told Peter not to get friendly with the Joes, knowledge of their real identities would only increase their risk of compromise. The only contact permitted was to show them how to get in and out of the aircraft.

'Hello there, I'm Peter Denhay. I'll be flying you tonight, shall I show you the ropes?'

'Certainly. Thank you.' Peter noticed the man's faint French accent.

'Been in before?'

'No.'

'Then it's a first time for both of us,' Peter winked. 'Don't worry, you're in safe hands.'

*

Eve had always thought that the best time to visit Paris was Spring. June was far too humid. But Paris had changed immensely since her last visit before the war. For one, there was a marked increase in German uniforms that seemed to populate every café or restaurant. They crowded into the *Folies-Belleville* or stumbled drunk from the lowliest brothels, reeking of cheap perfume. They were everywhere, like great rats. Their occupation of France had not improved it. Paris had become a giant rest centre and their policy as overlord was to suck the country's resources dry to pay for their war. Rationing was the only thing that was widespread, as people joked; coal was hard to come by and petrol impossible. More worrying still, she had heard tell of the arrest and persecution of Jews.

She sipped her coffee in a small tabac on the Rue du Chevet, a pleasant suburban street in the 11th Arrondissement, and reflected on her mission so far. Her immediate priority upon arrival, more than a week ago now, had been to find lodgings. Luckily, those Parisians who could emigrate to the country had done so and accommodation was in ready supply. A few enquiries led her to a boarding house near Montparnasse Station run by a widow who was prepared to let a squalid room in her attic for a scandalous sum. Madame Foulon's husband had not returned from the last war and, though she clearly believed Eve was one of the many prostitutes drawn to the garrison by the occupation. She talked passionately about her hatred of *Les Boches*, chain-smoking throughout. Eve liked the proud, indefatigable Frenchwoman immediately.

A pair of German soldiers entered the tabac, mere boys really. One smiled at her and she looked away pointedly. She had sat there all morning, observing the property across the street that contained Stephen Plainfare's flat. As the afternoon passed, she noticed that no-one entered or left the building, a grim late-19th century edifice named La Maison Deauville. She was also watchful for anyone who seemed to linger or looked out of place. If Plainfare was in custody, then it was likely his residence was under surveillance too. She made up her mind to take a closer look, but that must wait until nightfall.

'Bonjour, mademoiselle.' Eve turned around to see one of the Germans miming the smoking of a cigarette. That was typical, she thought, only a Kraut would think bumming a cigarette off a pretty girl in a tabac was an appropriate prelude to intercourse.

'*Oui monsieur*,' Eve replied, taking her last cigarette from its pack, lighting it and sliding the empty carton towards the German. He looked confused. Eve slipped out as the other soldier laughed heartily at his friend's disappointment. She hurried down the street towards the Metro station without looking back, but took the precaution of ducking into a restaurant to check for potential tails. With more than a little satisfaction she saw that she had not been followed.

Later that evening she dropped over the wall behind La Maison Deauville. It was overgrown with weeds and the smell of decaying rubbish met her nostrils as she landed lightly in the garden. The property was shrouded in darkness and when she tried its handle, she found the backdoor locked. She gained access to a first-floor window by climbing onto the privy's roof and jimmied it open with a small crowbar. The sash lifted and she dropped headfirst into Plainfare's abode.

A loud creak from the floorboards caused her to freeze until she determined that it was her weight, and no other, that caused it. Straining to listen for any other presence in the flat, she took in her surroundings as her vision adjusted to the gloom. The flat was dusty and smelled of damp. An unmade bed stood in one corner of the room, a stained and battered mattress upon it. In the adjacent room, which served jointly as kitchen, bathroom, and living room, a broken chair laid next to a lonely table set with smashed crockery. It was impossible to tell whether these were signs of a struggle or merely the detritus of long neglect. What was clear was that the Grapple network was not masterminded from this place, and S.O.E was apparently blind to that.

Through the windows on the street-side of the building, Eve peered out on the *Rue De Chevet* itself. It was blacked out and silent at this time of night. Her eyes, perfectly attuned to the dark by now, collected no movement in the shadows. She thought there was a faint flicker of a curtain in the house across the road, but when she stared at the window it remained unmoved. She didn't think she'd imagined it and so decided to slip out the back again. At the open sash, she cast a final look about the flat and wondered where Plainfare was, if not here. It did not look like he would return soon either.

*

The ringing of a telephone in his house behind the Place de la Concorde intruded upon Stolcher's reverie. It had once belonged to a wealthy Jewish family, but he'd had them moved on elsewhere without their bourgeois artworks or fine furnishings. Officially the residence was the headquarters of Operational BALDUR and housed the small team he had selected to run his counter-intelligence mission. Unofficially, aside from the two large rooms allocated to his staff, it was his private residence and could be accessed by a separate staircase gained through an inconspicuous door at the rear of the property.

It was up this staircase that Stolcher had ushered the two young ladies he was entertaining tonight with a dinner brought over specially from *La Coupole*. They *were* young, he reflected, but they were not ladies; he preferred it that way. He had picked up Mariette and Claudine working in a cheap bistro nearby.

'Can I help you to some more of this delightful bouillabaisse, my dear? More wine perhaps?'

The girls giggled appreciatively and Stolcher smiled, his loins stirred at the sound.

'Must you answer the telephone, Erich?'

Stolcher tilted his head, there was no let-up in the ringing. He glanced at the capacious feast on the table, and then at his company. He cursed duty and threw down his napkin.

He snatched the receiver from the telephone in the hallway and answered tersely. It was Guhr calling from Avenue Foch, who told him that someone had been in the flat at La Maison Deauville.

'You tailed him? Where did he go?'

There was a pause on the other end of the line, Guhr was clearly picking his next words carefully.

'Regrettably, Herr Hauptsturmfuhrer, the surveillance team was not in place. It took time to organise. When they arrived, they found the flat empty.'

'Where are the others?'

'They are on that job tonight. Remember? Near Amiens.'

'*Dummköpfe*. I entrust one simple task to the fucking Carlingue and they screw it up. Swap out the teams at the other locations. Yes, yes, I know it will require more people. I'll square it with the boss in the morning. And Guhr? Don't breathe a word of this to anyone,' Stolcher hissed and slammed down the receiver without waiting for a reply.

He was so furious that he couldn't even enjoy the excellent '33 Burgundy in his hand. He had given the Carlingue, the French auxiliary Gestapo, the basic donkey work of this operation and they had let him down. That was the last time he'd make that mistake, he decided. It was entirely possible that an intruder in the flat could have been a thief or a vagrant, but Stolcher had not risen to his present position by dismissing coincidence. He knew, better than anyone else, that BALDUR's strength was that he controlled all the agents in the network. If there was someone snooping around, then the British might uncover the fact that Plainfare was languishing in Fresnes Prison with most of his fellow agents, and his wireless was sending false messages to London. If his plan was blown, his reputation would be down the pan too. He needed to catch whoever this was, and quick.

'Erich,' Claudine called from the open dining room door, 'Are you there? I heard you shouting. Whatever is the matter?'

Stolcher smoothed his hair and flashed a smile, 'Yes, *lieb*. I'm at your service. Just a small problem at work.' He placed an arm around her and steered her back to the table away from the rooms in which the secrets of Operation BALDUR were laid bare. He treated himself to a lingering glance at her bosom as he did so, letting out an unconscious sigh.

'We thought it might be your wife,' Mariette said with a smile. 'Calling to tell you she's coming to join you.' Both girls laughed at this.

'No, not my wife.' Stolcher took a mouthful of wine and shook his head. 'She absolutely loathes Paris.'

*

Peter levelled out at the top of the climb out from Tangmere and swung onto his new course. In the bright moonlight he could easily identify the Seven Sisters receding to his left and the broad expanse of the channel below. The waves were silvery ripples 500 feet beneath the aeroplane and a light wisp of cloud hung in the air above. Otherwise, the sky was clear. His chart, cut up into panels covering the route out and back, rested on his left knee and he flew the aircraft comfortably with his right hand. The gentle breeze against his cheek turned cold. He closed the cockpit window and settled in for the flight. Whistling *The Jumpin' Jive* unconsciously, he peered into the night.

It was vitally important that he made his first turn accurately because the remainder of the route depended on it. There was a gap in the German flak defences between Le Tréport and Abbeville. Missing that gap even by a mile or two might put him in a flak gunner's sights. He pushed the wireless transmit button and called Blackgang radar station on the Isle of Wight.

'Hello Blackgang, this is Pimpernel. How now "Cabot"? Over.' Blackgang's primary function was to steer RAF night fighters onto Luftwaffe intruders. But its radar could also provide accurate vectors for intruders going the other way, as it did now.

'Hello Pimpernel. Steer 03 port. Good luck, out.'

A thick belt of fog shrouded the enemy coast. Peter glanced at his stopwatch, ticking down the final few minutes before he must turn southwards to follow the route of the Somme. He climbed above it. The top was just above 2,000 feet and, looking over the fog bank to the interior, he saw the Somme twinkling back at him, snaking its way towards Amiens.

The Somme. That name was synonymous with so much bloodshed and loss in the last war. No schoolboy could hear it without picturing the blunting of the great combined French and British offensive of 1916. Kitchener's Army, Fricourt, Thiepval, Fromelles. The Somme had impeded movement and turned the entire landscape into a glutinous misery. But here, in its lower reaches, it guided him along gently towards his terminus.

North of Amiens the river ran unnaturally straight for a mile. Not far, but distinct enough for the purpose of navigation. He was above the feature before he realised. He reset the stopwatch and pushed the rudder bar hard right to turn directly south. Three minutes. Three minutes and he would be above the landing ground. He looked up over the nose where he expected to see the three lights shining in an inverted 'L' shape to mark the field. The procedure was that the lights would blink at his approach and he would reply by flashing his landing lights in the Morse code for his aircraft letter. One minute and 29 seconds. Nothing. His mouth ran dry as a sickening feeling of doubt crept in. Peter glanced at his map, looking for an error he might have made and finding none.

Peter eased back the throttle and let the nose come up slightly as he searched all around the cockpit for evidence of a reception party. The Lysander's Mercury engine burbled confidently with the airspeed sitting at 80 mph. Lights appeared in the greyness below, further off than Peter expected, but unmistakable. They were firm and unblinking, contrary to the agreed exchange of signals. He switched the landing light on once for a beat of three seconds, then flashed it three times. The ground lights remained steady.

Strictly speaking, he should turn the aircraft northwards now and return to Tangmere to report a misidentification. But the Resistance occasionally messed up their signals; they weren't professional aerodrome operators. Failing to deliver the Joe on his first operational sortie was likely to attract criticism too. For a moment he hung there riven with indecision, all the time the lights rushed towards him. His gut told him to go for it.

The engine rattled as Peter pushed the throttle forward; he was committed now. Over the top of the lights he pulled into a gentle turning descent, intending to land parallel to the long side of the 'L'. He would then taxi back to the touch-down point where the reception party awaited him. A glance into the darkness below revealed nothing untoward.

The altimeter's needle pointed to 200 feet exactly when the 'L' reappeared in the forward cockpit glass, flatter and foreshortened now. The Lysander handled beautifully, he thought, and not for the first time. She was a grand old girl, a duchess. The airspeed drained away and Peter held the nose up. A reassuring thump told him the flaps and slats had extended. The lights disappeared as the engine cowling extinguished them. A moment of anxiety followed when everything went silent and then there was a startling bump as the landing gear hit the grass. He glimpsed the flash of a light past the wing and pressed the brakes hard, chopping the throttle back to idle.

The Lysander was rolling at a fast taxi 150 yards later when the second lamp appeared level with the cockpit. Peter lowered the port window, admitting cooling air and the sweet aroma of burnt aviation fuel. He braked the right wheel and turned about the outer lamp towards where he had first touched down. It occurred to him that he had forgotten to switch on the landing light in the last 100 feet. He did so now and sent a powerful beam of light scything across the field.

His eyes hardly believed the sight in front of him. Where he had expected a small group of people clustered around the first lamp, the landing light picked out a thin skirmish line of something like 30 men. Some carried electric flashlights, others held dogs on a tight leash, but all were armed, and all wore German field grey. The realisation came to Peter in a flash. A second more told him there was insufficient room or time to turn into wind and make a bid for freedom. The knowledge he would be captured, and his passenger shot, brought a sick feeling to his stomach.

Peter slammed the throttle forward to its stop and the engine spooled up again with its characteristic pop and rattle. The Lysander bumped along the ground as its speed increased to a run. The line of soldiers halted. Not wishing to be run bodily over, those directly in the aircraft's path broke first, running or leaping out of the way. But some on the outer ends of the line opened fire and rounds punched into the airframe around the cockpit and elsewhere. The cockpit's side window shattered, and Peter felt something strike him about the ear. He barely registered the intense burning sensation until the aircraft leapt from the grass airfield and climbed steeply into the night sky.

Peter cursed himself for breaking regulations, it was damned fool thing to do. He studied the instruments, several of which were smashed and unresponsive including the altimeter and, more alarmingly, the compass. Wind billowed in through the smashed side window and chilled the sweat that had poured from him in the last couple of minutes. He reached up to touch his right ear and discovered that his leather helmet was torn open. When he withdrew his hand, it was damp and tacky with blood. The same wetness seeped into his collar and down his shirt. A dizzy sensation overwhelmed him, and he fought to remain conscious and to think.

All was not lost; he had engine power and the aircraft remained aloft. By taking off on the reciprocal of his landing direction, he knew he was heading roughly south-west and he just needed to put the moon on the other side of the aircraft to attain a northerly course. The turn did not bring the silver ribbon of the Somme into view, but instead it revealed a thick bank of cloud that crept towards him ominously, blotting out the landscape from one wingtip to the other. Peter was staggered by the rapidity with which it had built, only belatedly remembering to climb above it Entering a fogbank without instruments was suicidal.

The blanket of white extended beneath him, on one hand bringing safety from light flak but on the other blotting out any hope of finding the marks to steer him home. The landing light illuminated the cloud, highlighting his position to any airborne prowlers and he leaned forward sharply to extinguish it.

With a deep breath he pushed the wireless transmit button and said, 'Come in Blackgang, mayday, mayday. Pimpernel mayday. Over.'

Silence. He waited and prayed. If the wireless was damaged, he was truly buggered. He made to press the button again when his earphones crackled.

'Hello Pimpernel, what's your emergency? Over.'

'Instrument failure. I need a way home.'

'Stand-by for course to steer, Pimpernel.'

'That won't do Blackgang, my compass is out too.'

There was a pause. Peter pictured the scene in the radar station's control room as the duty controller worked out how to deal with his pickle. In the chilled darkness of the cockpit, he shivered and thought about Eve. She was likely alone and possibly in danger too. The preposterous idea that he should marry her if he survived this trial manifested in his mind. He dismissed it.

'Come in Pimpernel. Maintain course and speed, stand-by for further instructions. Blackgang out.'

The wireless snapped off again, leaving him with the whistling of the wind and the deep roar of the engine. He was no wiser to the plan. In any case, he could not communicate this to his passenger because there was no intercom to connect him to the rear compartment. Somewhere below, the land was giving way to the water of the Channel. He had no option but to continue on roughly northwards, ignorant of whether he was heading to Dover or Penzance. He tapped the petrol gauge, stuck resolutely on half-full, and hoped the tank hadn't been holed.

He became aware of a shadow closing in above him some 15 minutes later. It covered the stars above the canopy and swept in front of the Lysander, resolving itself into the definitive outline of a twin-engine aircraft. A sleek and fast fighter, he guessed, by the speed with which it overtook him. The only light it emitted was the faint glow from its exhaust cowlings. It bled off speed until it sat comfortably 50 yards ahead and above him. A brief flash of its navigation lights and the aircraft eased into a slow left-hand turn. Peter smiled to himself through the throbbing pain. Blackgang had sent a shepherd; he was being guided home.

Relief flooded his mind. It was followed by Eve again. The absurd memory of their day at the Roman villa near Chearney, the sincere look on her face when she talked about archaeology, and the way she laughed at his stupid jokes. He would survive this; he *would* ask for her hand in marriage. The lead aircraft started its descent. Peter was unsure how long he'd been flying since they'd joined, but the fog was breaking up below him. There was the sea glinting again and, much further away, the dark grey mass of home.

A dozen points of light burned their way through the darkness and RAF Tangmere's flarepath materialised in the distance, twinkling brightly As if in a dream, Peter reduced the throttle and turned towards the lights. His shepherd detached, reappearing a short time later on his wing. Together, they descended towards the airfield, 500, 400, 300 feet. The light of the flarepath grew in intensity and then the guide waggled his wings and climbed away, his job done. Peter waved him an affectionate, albeit unseen, goodbye.

The Lysander landed with a jolt, bounced, and touched down again. Peter turned off the flarepath and let the aircraft roll to a halt before shutting down. The ringing bells of the station's fire engines reached his ears when the propeller stopped spinning and he patted his tunic in search of the cigarettes he had left in a wooden box in the operations hut. He had no idea how long it was before Colin appeared at the open window, peering in with a shocked look on his face.

'How are you, old man? Looks as if you've had quite a time of it,' Colin said.

'I've had better trips,' Peter replied, removing his helmet.

'Oh Christ, you've been knocked about too.'

'Is it bad?'

'Half an inch to the right and it'd be a whole lot worse,' Colin grinned. 'But we ought to get it looked at.'

Peter clambered down from the Lysander's high cockpit, finding his legs like jelly. His hands shook uncontrollably. He thrust them inside his Mae West to keep them out of sight of the engineers and firefighters who had responded to his mayday call.

'Ambulance? Where's the ambulance crew?' Colin shouted at the mass of people surrounding the aeroplane.

'We don't need an ambulance, Colin. It's only a scratch,' Peter exclaimed. But Colin nodded back at the Lysander, where a party was lowering the Joe from the rear compartment. The scene struck instantly at Peter's heart because, from the way he sagged in their arms and flopped onto the proffered stretcher, it was obvious that his passenger was quite dead.

Chapter Eight

The man gazing back at Charlie in the mirror of his cell was not one he recognised. *His* eyes were small, beady orbs and his skin faintly grey. He had not been permitted shaving things, so coarse stubble covered his chin and cheeks. Nevertheless, he straightened his tie and smoothed his unruly black hair in preparation for going before the Groupie, for what he expected was to hear the date of his impending court-martial.

Behind the door marked 'Station Commander' sat a man not much older than Charlie, or so he looked. Charlie knew nothing about it him, other than that he had been a well-regarded bomber squadron commander and had won an Air Force Cross for bringing a badly mauled Wellington back from the Ruhr.

'Ah, Kendrick, don't sit down; this won't take long. Fighting, I understand?'

'Yes sir,' Charlie replied.

'Well it's a damned bad thing. Imagine if everyone walloped their squadron boss just because they didn't get on with him. What sort of weak-minded crowd of nitwits would we be if we overlooked this, eh?'

Charlie said nothing. There was really nothing to say. The Station Commander continued in his odd, upbeat tone.

'So, I've no choice but to transfer you to operations. With immediate effect.'

'Operations, sir?'

'Yes Kendrick, operations. You know, against Germany.'

'There's not to be a court-martial then, sir?'

'I dare say there ought to be, but a friend of yours intervened.' The Station Commander looked about for some paperwork on his desk and eventually found it. 'Wing Commander Corbett. D'you know him?'

'He was my first squadron commander, sir.'

'Well he's got 75 (New Zealand) Squadron now and it seems he's keen to have you on one of his crews.'

'That's wonderful news, sir,' Charlie replied with unmistakable joy. It was almost too good to be true.

'Remarkable, isn't it?

'Oh yes.' Charlie wondered if there was a certain droll tone in the Station Commander's voice, like he believed it was more than just remarkable.

'Kendrick. Before you skip off out of here, can I offer you some advice? First, I know that you're enough of a man not to gloat about side-stepping a trial. But it would be an awful, low thing to throw this back in Squadron Leader Chappell's face, so to speak. Second, you might reflect on the fact that you have jumped successfully from the frying pan, only to land directly in the fire.' The Station Commander shook his head, 'When are you lot going to learn to save the real blows for Jerry?'

RAF Feltwell was located just west of Thetford in East Anglia. It was home to a couple of 3 Group's bomber squadrons equipped with the Vickers Wellington. Both were warned-off for operations tonight, and the sun rose over an airfield alive with activity as the serviceable airframes were refuelled and bombed-up. Their orders had been created at Headquarters Bomber Command at High Wycombe that morning. They had been called through to 3 Group Headquarters based at Harraton House in Suffolk, who selected the stations to provide the striking force.

Men from 75 (New Zealand) Squadron crowded outside the Station Briefing Room to receive their orders and that was where Charlie met his new crew. The Skipper, 'Cobber' Benstead, introduced them to him in order: Wireless Operator,

Nose-Gunner and Tail Gunner. Bewildered by the events of the previous 24 hours, Charlie instantly forgot their names. A lone Englishman in a full Kiwi crew, he felt strangely isolated despite Cobber's warm welcome. The hubbub was all about where they would go tonight, and whispered conversations sought to guess the likely target. The Ruhr was always a reliable destination, but good odds could be had for the Big City too, as Berlin was known.

He trooped into the dark, utilitarian theatre with the others and sat alongside his crew in a row of uncomfortable wooden seats. The room filled with the heady smell of tobacco, body odour and serge uniforms. He'd attended countless briefings like this. Still, his head thumped with the return of his anxiety and he tried to disguise it by placing his hand against his forehead and squeezing his temples. The noise of nearly 100 men chatting and laughing was replaced with stony silence as Feltwell's Station Commander entered and drew back the curtains to reveal the target. Benstead gave an audible sigh of relief and elbowed Charlie in the ribs.

'Brest. It's a milk-run, mate,' he whispered. 'No night fighters, cock-all flak. *You* can come again.'

When the briefing broke up, Charlie made his way to the front where Johnny Corbett stood conversing with a couple of other senior officers. He'd changed very little since Greece. Tall and spare with dark hair, greying about the temples, he smiled grimly at Charlie's approach.

'Ah, Kendrick, I heard you were in town. Welcome to 75 Squadron,' Corbett boomed, gripping his hand.

'Thank you, sir. And thank you for requesting my transfer.'

'Oh, that was nothing to do with me. Your chum Denhay sent me a message. Didn't he say anything about it?'

Charlie was speechless to hear that Peter had even bothered to look him up after their last conversation.

'It must have slipped his mind.'

'You've got a good friend there. Well, you'll have to tell me some other time about how you two managed to get out of Greece. Awful news about the rest of the chaps.' Corbett thumped him on the arm in a friendly way and walked off. It *was* awful how XXI Squadron had been thrown away in Greece, but nobody dwelled for long on the men who'd gone to fly operations on the other side of the immortal plane.

*

Lise Dubreys' address proved to be a tiny flat above an equally squat pharmacy in Montmarte, not far from the Place Pigelle. It was a sad-looking building, more like a backstreet abortionist's than the chemist's shop it purported to be. Eve had visited it twice before, both times to watch from afar. Dubreys was at least alive, and apparently free. She left the flat twice a day, once to visit a dead-drop location that was known to S.O.E., and again to walk in a local park. Eve had not seen her in the company of anyone else and neither had she observed anyone other than Dubreys enter or leave the flat.

Normally, Eve would have waited longer before contacting Dubreys. After all, it took weeks, months sometimes, to build up an accurate idea of the pattern of life surrounding a mark, and Eve had only been in France just over a fortnight. But she had not sent a single message back to Sutherland so far, and Dubreys had a functioning wireless. A twinge reminded her there was also something else to consider.

Eve leaned against the wall to steady herself as the feeling of nausea threatened to overwhelm her. She swallowed hard, hoping she would not vomit here in the street like she had the other morning. A cold sweat broke out across her body and the foul taste of bile filled her mouth. She spat, then straightened up and blinked away the tears in her eyes. It had been like this almost every day since she had arrived, over a week ago. She could not be certain, but her intuition told her she was pregnant.

Eve had no strong desire to experience motherhood. It wasn't that she was vehemently against it, just that it was something she'd never planned to do. Though there was no definitive proof that she was carrying a baby, her willingness to entertain the prospect surprised her. She certainly felt a renewed sense of responsibility, but the thought that occupied France was no place for an expectant mother gnawed at her. In turn, there was a growing anxiety that the values she held so strongly as an operative were being undermined.

For the umpteenth time she patted her coat pocket that concealed her pistol, then she crossed the street and let herself into the hallway that led up to Dubreys' flat. The door opened to reveal typical Parisian decay, chipped floor tiles and flaking paint. She drew the door latch across and climbed the stairs to the first-floor landing, where she knocked firmly on the door. The floorboards creaked and then she heard footsteps on the other side. *Dubreys wears shoes inside*, she said to herself. It was a fact, à propos of nothing.

The door opened a fraction and Eve found herself face-to-face with the woman whose photo she had first seen in London. She looked thinner now and careworn. She squinted suspiciously around the door.

'*Oui? Puis-je vous aider?*'

'You can help me by letting me in. I've been sent by London,' Eve replied.

'I wasn't expecting anyone,' Lise said, closing the door quickly behind Eve. Her words were heavily accented.

'When was your last communication?'

'A few days ago now. I asked for an additional wireless operator to be sent out.'

'Why, is there something wrong with your set?'

'No. It's because-' Lise paused. 'Who are you anyway?

'I was sent by Ivor Jones,' Eve said. 'To help develop Grapple.'

'But there was no word of this, how did you get here?'

'There's no time to explain all this. I need to use your wireless. Where is it please?'

'The bedroom. A panel behind the bed.'

Eve followed Lise into the only other room in the flat. A glance out of the window revealed they were not overlooked. Below the window a wrought iron shade jutted out into a pokey yard.

Whilst Lise set up the suitcase wireless set, Eve returned to the kitchen and scribbled down her message, transcribing it into code from memory. It was a simple cipher technique called a Poem Code. She had used it many times before. There was an intentional error included within it that acted as a security check. The poem Sunderland had given her was *Invictus* by William Ernest Henly. She smiled to herself as she remembered the words of the all-important final lines:

It matters not how strait the gate,
How charged with punishment the scroll,
I am the master of my fate,
I am the captain of my soul.

It was the sort of beautiful tosh they'd taught at whatever school Sutherland had been sent to, but her experience had taught her that it had real meaning.

'I can send this for you,' Lise said, peering over her shoulder.

'No. Thank you. Perhaps you would be good enough to fetch me a drink?'

'Would you like a cognac?'

'Water will be fine. Thank you.'

The suitcase set rested on the narrow bed. Its aerial disappeared into the loft above and was craftily concealed inside the body of the light fitting in the ceiling when not connected. Eve pulled the earphones on, leaving one earcup above her left ear so that she was not completely deaf. She tapped the message out quickly, holding the thin message paper in her left hand. The entire process took her less than three minutes, by which time Lise returned with a glass of tap water.

Eve removed the earphones and, smiling, reached out to take the glass from Lise's trembling hand. She froze. Only a brief glance at Lise's face told her she had been betrayed, even before the crack of the downstairs door being kicked in reached her ears. Running footsteps on the stairs caused her heart to beat wildly. Eve crammed the message paper in her mouth and chewed as the inner door thumped open.

The first man into the room carried a Luger but never used it. Eve squeezed the Colt's trigger and sent two slugs into him. He collapsed onto the floor with a muffled groan. Lise screamed and broke for the door but ran directly into automatic fire sprayed wildly through the doorway from the landing. Eve fired a couple more shots to keep the intruders' heads down and then hurled the suitcase set through the bedroom window, smashing it wide open. She did not stop to look back, but threw herself feet first through the open aperture, slid down the iron porch below, and landed in a crouch in the yard, completely unhurt.

'*Achtung! Hände hoch*,' shouted a leather-coated man in the yard. Other men pressed in from the alleyway beyond. There was no way out. Eve stared down the barrel of a machine-pistol and cursed. Reluctantly, she stood and lifted her hands above her head.

*

'Just a little light flak everyone. No need to worry.'

Charlie smiled at Benstead's drawl over the intercom. In the screened-off navigator's station behind the cockpit, he had no idea what 'a little light flak' looked like to Benstead. But it felt heavy enough to him as it jolted and rocked the aircraft. He could hear it bursting over the drone of the bomber's twin engines. Their position was towards the rear of the bomber force attacking Brest. Consequently, he could tell the anti-aircraft gunners were thoroughly awake by the crack of exploding shells that echoed through the metal tube in which he rode. He checked the clock again, glanced at the line on the map and said, 'Navigator to Skipper, stand-by for Initial Point in five minutes.'

The Initial Point marked the start of the bomb run, which ran from east to west, so that any mis-drops went into the roadstead and not into the city. In theory. At 15,000 feet it was a challenge to even find, let alone hit, a target the size of a dockyard at night. There was also an unexpectedly strong northerly wind he had to correct for, and Charlie had no bombing aids to assist him.

'Make your heading 275 degrees,' Charlie said.

'275 degrees, navigator. The aircraft is yours,' Benstead replied.

Charlie hauled himself out of the cramped station and shuffled forward under the cockpit to the nose. It took some effort because he was encumbered with the bulk of his flying clothing, as well as his parachute. He crawled to the bomb-aimer's position, where a glass panel in the nose gave him a panoramic view of the battle unfolding before his eyes. What he saw caused him to gasp in shock.

Ahead and below, an enormous fire loomed out of the night, which was back lit with an eerie orange glow. This must be the docks. The earth was so thick with smoke that it seethed. Ground fire rose into the sky in great arcs, travelling slowly at first, then speeding up as it approached and disappeared above him. The acrid smell of cordite from the flak bursts met his nose. In amongst the city there were dozens of pinpricks of light, signs that the RAF's incendiaries had not fallen exclusively within the docks, and where incendiaries had fallen, so must the bombs.

Charlie shook his head in disbelief and told himself bombing accuracy could not possibly be this bad. As he did so, he realised sadly that the Germans could never light as many decoy fires as this.

'How's it looking navigator?'

Charlie was called back to the present. The wind was blowing them off track to the south.

'Hello Skipper. Hard right or we're going to miss it.'

'Roger.'

The aircraft slipped, but the dock fire remained well to the right of the nose.

'No, it won't do. We'll not make it on this heading. We're going to have to go around Skipper.'

'Can't you just dump the load now? I really don't fancy going back through that again, navigator.'

'I've no idea what's down there. I'm not dropping on civilians, Skipper.'

In the pause that followed, everyone listened expectantly for Benstead's reply. Charlie knew that no-one wanted to chance another run through alert enemy defences; they must be cursing him right now. But on the other hand, he had a responsibility to ensure their payload landed on a legitimate target. Regardless of the evidence to the contrary.

The engines spooled up again and Charlie felt the aircraft tilt to port, away from England, beginning a left-handed turn to take them back to the start of the bomb-run. He grinned to himself, *good old Cobber*. From memory, this turn would take them over the undefended Crozon Peninsula, before joining the Initial Point again somewhere north of Daoulas. The flak lessened; he relaxed. Perhaps he would get on alright with this crew after all.

Charlie was thrown sideways as a tremendous explosion rocked the aircraft, causing his ears to ring. He smelled burning metal and tasted copper in his mouth, the bomber was on fire. Flickering shadows on the inside of the fuselage told him it was the port wing. He shouted into the intercom, 'Everyone ok?' There was no reply. Cursing, he pulled off his helmet and told the nose gunner he was going to speak with the skipper.

Benstead was slumped sideways in his seat, his face frozen in death. Whatever had punched through the port wing had enough explosive force to do for him too. But Charlie had no time to reflect because the heat of the flames engulfing the fuselage stung his face and forced him to kneel. He snatched up Benstead's microphone and told everyone to bail out. One last glance back down the fuselage revealed the fire was spreading fast.

Ducking back into the nose, Charlie saw that the gunner was fitting his parachute to its harness. The cramped turret was not large enough to permit him to wear it at his guns.

'Get out,' Charlie shouted in a strange and high-pitched voice. Then the bomb bay exploded.

The force of the blast that ruptured the aircraft must have knocked Charlie out for a moment, because when he came to, he was pressed into the bomb-aimer's position in the nose, which was no longer attached to the aeroplane. He heard the whistling first, the sound of the nose section free-falling through the night sky, and then the frantic screams of the anonymous nose-gunner. The fellow was gripping onto the torn and jagged fuselage with one gloved hand and he stared at Charlie in alarm and desperation. Charlie reached out to him, holding onto the stringers to stop himself from being whipped away. Leaning as far as he could reach, his hand was still just shy of the gunner's. He stretched further, his body groaned with the effort, but the gunner's grip failed and the man was cast off into the darkness, disappearing in an instant.

The stars above his head swung gently, the wreckage spun as it is plummeted towards the earth. He pulled himself to the edge and waited. When the stars reappeared, he took a great gulp, closed his eyes and threw himself into the void. There was a thump on his foot as the nose section caught his flying boot and then he too was in freefall and probing frantically for his ripcord. He found it and jerked it hard.

Charlie was snatched up by his shoulders and groin as the parachute deployed, knocking the wind out of him. He swung once, twice and with great surprise felt vegetation brushing against his body. Branches rustled and snapped as he passed through what felt like a tree, to land with a heavy thump below. The darkness pressed in all around him, and he felt its unremitting embrace.

Chapter Nine

France, August 1941

Jumbo Sutherland took a deep draw on his cigarette and surveyed the towering pile of buff-coloured files on his desk with distaste. Heavy drumming of rain on his office window told him that British summer had arrived in full force. Other than reflecting that he had forgotten his umbrella, he paid it no heed. Sutherland's attention was entirely focused on a file that arrived only moments before, borne by one of the building's many discreet messengers. The file was marked TOP SECRET - BIGOT.

BIGOT stood for British Invasion of German Occupied Territory and signified the importance of the intelligence contained within. He slid the others to one side and flipped it open. The smell of dried, musty paper met his nostrils. Inside were a series of decrypts, wireless messages received in code and translated back into plain text by an unknown cryptanalyst at Bletchley Park.

Helpfully, as well as providing a full transcript of the message, the cryptanalyst included a delicately hand-written note detailing their observations on the message. Through force of habit, Sutherland left this part to read last. He flipped the paper over and studied the typed message, the first he had received from Eve since being dropped in France over a month ago. It told him little. She had arrived safe, had concerns over Grapple, was unable to locate the network's organiser, and intended to send a more thorough report in the coming fortnight.

He turned back to the accompanying note and read it several times. Something felt wrong but he couldn't quite place it. An intense hot pain in his fingertips signalled his fingers were burning. With a jump, he remembered his cigarette and stubbed it out on a saucer with a silent oath. The cryptanalyst referred to a mistake in the penultimate line of Eve's message where an indecipherable set of letters had appeared. In the cryptanalyst's estimation, the word the operator intended to use was 'send'. Sutherland was untroubled by this, there was supposed to be a mistake in the penultimate line of the message. This was a check he had agreed with Eve, which told him the message had not been sent under duress or altered during its transmission. What worried Sutherland was the line that followed.

It was a simple sentence, but it opened a window somewhere in Sutherland's mind that looked out onto a troubled landscape. The sentence ran: *A mistake of this nature is uncharacteristic of GRAPPLE operators, whose messages are of uniform excellent quality.* That singular statement did not ring true. In fact, the often rushed and sometimes hunted wireless operators of S.O.E. routinely sent error-riddled messages. So, Sutherland had to ask himself, *why was Grapple any different?*

His first thought was that the cryptanalyst was just plain wrong or had confused the mistake with the security checks used by S.O.E.'s F-Section. He grabbed the telephone receiver and asked for the department at Bletchley that dealt with his cipher traffic. He pictured one of many green telephones ringing in the huts encircling the stately home that handled the most secretive of the country's communications and code-breaking functions. A woman answered.

'Ciphers. Petty Officer Wren Standish speaking.'

'Hello, Lieutenant Colonel Sutherland here. Can you scramble?'

'One moment please,' Standish replied. The receiver went silent for a moment.

'Are we scrambled?'

'Yes sir, all set. How may I help?'

'I've been looking over a Grapple signal you decrypted for me and I had a question about something in the cryptanalyst's note.'

'That's Marion's desk. I'll fetch her.'

'Thank you.' Sutherland drummed his fingers impatiently as he waited for Marion to come to the telephone. These women were the experts, he knew, there was no sense calling a faceless staff officer for an answer when he could go straight to the originator. He had always preferred short lines.

'Hello sir, Leading Wren Barker here. I understand you had a question about some Grapple traffic?'

'In your note you said that the messages from Grapple wireless operations are "of uniform excellent quality". Did you mean apart from the security checks?'

'Grapple operators don't use security checks, sir.'

'I beg your pardon?'

Sutherland was stunned; he listened in disbelief. The security checks, a random set of characters at the beginning and end of each signal, were the only mechanism that S.O.E. possessed to verify the authenticity of an agent's message. To any responsible agent handler, a transmission without security checks was at best untrustworthy. At worst, it was an invitation to send countless numbers of people to their deaths.

'S.O.E. told us to ignore missing security checks on Grapple messages,' Barker explained, 'They said their wireless operators routinely forget them, and we should treat it as common practice for this network.'

'Who gave this order?'

'Captain Kingham, from F-Section.'

'And the messages you've received from Grapple, can you judge whether they're from one operator or a number of operators?'

'Oh, they've all got a tell, sir. I'd say that it's a single operator. Flawless transmissions, although occasionally heavy-handed on some vowels.'

'And how does that compare with traffic you've seen from other wireless operators?'

'Well, it's unusual to see so few mistakes, of course. Perhaps the operator composes the messages well in advance and practices them before transmission?'

'I see. Thank you for your time.'

'Was that all, sir?'

'Yes. For now. Goodbye.'

Sutherland replaced the receiver and stared out of the window where the rain was easing. Icy fingers played up his spine, the feeling he always got when he'd taken a misstep. He shook his head angrily, the answer to the Head's question had been at his fingertips all along. To prove it, however, he would need to work quickly indeed. And if he was right, he realised with a start, then he had as good as signed Eve Moore's death warrant.

*

Charlie awoke as if from a deep slumber, to the touch of wet grass against his face. The scent of ripe apples recalled him to his senses. *I'm alive,* he told himself. With a groan, he rolled onto his back and glanced skyward where his parachute risers disappeared into a tangle of branches and silk. A high morning sun filtered down through the trees, lending a greenish tint to the light. His senses told him he had landed in an orchard. A French orchard, his brain reminded him with a start. The Germans must have seen a burning aircraft descending over land last night. They would, even now, be combing the countryside thereabouts for wreckage. For survivors.

The moment of panic passed abruptly, and he was again master of himself. His duty was clear, he must evade capture and make his way back to fight again. But he had no idea where he was, or how he might remain at large in a country occupied by the enemy. He told himself not to worry about the journey, but rather concentrate on the first step. He popped the locking wheel on his parachute harness and sat up gingerly. Brushing wet leaves off his face, he reflected that, other than the ever-present dull thumping in his temples, he appeared to be more or less intact. He rose to his knees and then stood unsteadily, waiting for the dizzy spell to pass.

The orchard appeared to run for several hundred yards in every direction and was ringed by a low stone wall. To one end, above the wall, he glimpsed a golden wheat field and another small block of trees beyond it. Walking towards this, he came upon a wooden gate and a girl staring back at him. Charlie froze and stared back. She was caught in the act of collecting apples. Indeed, a dozen or so large red and green examples rested in the cotton pinny she wore over simple working clothes. She yelped in surprise, dropped her apples and shot into a sunken lane the gate opened onto. Charlie forgot his shyness and chased after her trying to remember schoolboy French and shouting, 'Mademoiselle, mademoiselle. I mean no harm.'

He rounded the gatepost and almost ran onto the prongs of a pitchfork brandished in his face.

'My dear,' Charlie said, raising his hands in surrender, 'I'm an Englishman. *Je suis anglais*.'

'*Anglais*?'

'Very much so. D'you speak any English? My name's Charlie.'

'Charlie?' She pronounced it 'Sharlay', which made him smile. Her words were heavily accented, but she spoke clearly when she replied, '-a little. Only a little English.'

Charlie regarded her. Her face, initially scrunched up in a look of fierce aggression, now relaxed into an expression of curiosity. As it did so, Charlie realised she was not a girl at all, but in fact a young woman in her late teens or early twenties. She was a skinny, freckled thing with straw-coloured hair that flowed down her back tied in a ribbon. She was quite plain, but in a healthy, rosy-cheeked kind of way.

'If I promise not to escape, will you grant me parley?'

She looked surprised; the pitchfork dropped. Charlie turned to re-enter the orchard.

'Where are you going?'

'I caused you to drop your apples, I'm collecting them for you.'

She watched him pick them up one by one, arms folded, suspicion etched upon her face.

'What are they, Cookers?'

'I don't understand. The apples?'

When Charlie had gathered an armful, he offered them back to the girl who collected them again in her apron. She smiled demurely at his gesture.

'And do you have a name?'

The girl gazed at Charlie apprehensively for a moment, but her reply was cut off by a man's voice in the lane calling, 'Cecile, Cecile?'. Before Charlie could react, a young man appeared in the gateway. He gaped for a moment, then recovered and jabbered at Cecile in French, accompanied by dramatic pointing in Charlie's direction. He was gangly with greasy dark hair and signs of a patchy moustache. His face wore an exasperated and angry expression. Cecile replied forcefully and with a speed that Charlie could not follow, gesturing emphatically with both hands – the apples dropped again. Charlie stooped to take one and, biting into it, found it to be surprisingly soft and mild. The argument ended when the young man stamped his foot and, turning about on his heel, stalked off down the lane.

'That's Pascal Févre for you,' Cecile shrugged.

'Nice chap,' Charlie grinned, picking up the apples again. 'Friend of yours?'

'He works for my father, on our farm.'

'This is your place?'

'*Oui*. For what it's worth. My parents work it, I help them, and Pascal is our labourer.'

Charlie nodded to where the boy retreated, mumbling loudly to himself.

'What's his problem?'

'He thinks we should hand you over to the *Bosches*. He says you're trouble; you will bring trouble to us here.'

'What do *you* think?'

Cecile said nothing for a moment, then shook her head as if to dismiss whatever thought had occurred to her.

'Come meet Papa. He'll know what to do. We can't just give you up, it's unpatriotic.'

Charlie was relieved to hear it. He followed Cecile for a moment, then remembered his parachute remained stuck in the trees. Running back, Charlie tugged at the risers until the canopy eventually slid through the branches, releasing a torrent of apples. He bundled it up and then caught up with Cecile, who stood waiting in the lane. She led him in Pascal's footsteps towards a stone cottage perched on a little hillock in the distance. The cottage was flanked by a stone barn and surrounded by fields, which stretched away down the rolling hills in a patchwork of yellows and greens.

'It reminds me of Cornwall,' Charlie said.

'Cornwall?'

'It's a place across the Channel from here, we holidayed there when I was young. I can even smell the sea. Where are we? Near Brest?'

'This is Kerluen. Brest is to the north, across the water.'

'Goodness me. I've no idea how I ended up here. We were

trying to-' Charlie stopped mid-sentence as he realised he was about to say *bomb Brest.*

'Bomb Brest? We heard you last night, the bombers. It was so loud, and the sky was on fire. I've never seen anything like it in my life. What 'appened to you?'

'We were hit by flak. I think the fuel tank must have gone up or something.'

'What about your crew? Did any of them make it out?'

'I-, I don't think so,' Charlie replied after a while.

They walked the rest of the way in silence, Charlie lost in his thoughts. When they reached the cottage, Cecile let him into the kitchen through a rough wooden door. He was met by a couple he guessed were Cecile's parents. Pascal lurked in one corner and launched immediately into another tirade. This time directed at Cecile's father. Cecile added volubly to the discussion and Charlie stood awkwardly, still wrapped incongruously in the bulk of his parachute.

Cecile's father listened for a time with his arms folded. He glanced twice at Charlie, betraying nothing, and eventually spoke a few words to Pascal who fumed silently. With an evil look, he stormed out of the room.

'Charlie, this is my papa, Edouard Ropars, and maman, Lucille.'

'Delighted to meet you both.'

M. Ropars took Charlie's hand in his bearlike grip and spoke to him at length in French. He was not an old man, but a life working the land had imbued him with dark, leathery skin that suggested more advanced years. His wife was a slight, waiflike figure almost identical to Cecile in all but her eyes. Cecile's were a piercing bright blue, like her father's. Mme. Ropars smiled kindly at Charlie, when she had stopped staring at the large bundle of silk he carried. She poured a measure from a bottle into a glass for Charlie who, upon lifting it to his lips, discovered it was Cognac. It warmed him pleasantly as it travelled to his stomach and he closed his eyes, savouring the sensation.

'My father says you are welcome here. We will hide you until arrangements can be made to return you to England. He adds that there are severe penalties for hiding airmen. You must burn your uniform and act like a foreign labourer. You can work on the farm whilst he makes enquiries. There is a man in Quimper, who knows people that might help. But it will take time, Charlie. You could be here for months.'

'I understand,' Charlie replied. He was surprised, and then a little ashamed, to find that he did not burn with a strong desire to get home to fight. He sensed an expectant pause and said to M. Ropars, '*Merci Monsieur, merci beaucoup*.'

M. Ropars smiled at Charlie and said something in reply that made Cecile laugh.

'What is it?'

'He says you must avoid speaking French from now on.'

'Because I have to pretend to be a labourer?'

'Yes. And because your French is awful.'

*

'There you go, love. Neat as a pin.'

The pressure around Peter's neck lessened slightly as the nursing sister's hands came away from his bandage.

'Thank you,' Peter smiled through the pain. He was in uniform again after an overnight stay at Netley Hospital. The M.O. had insisted upon it when he inspected Peter's wound after landing at Tangmere.

'Now you mustn't be fiddling with that dressing,' Nurse Inglis went on, 'Doctor says you was lucky to get away with only half your ear gone. He told me that he could fair see the artery when he stitched you up. Don't you worry though, you're still a handsome devil.'

Peter flushed red and laughed awkwardly, wincing again with the pain.

'What happened to the chap opposite?'

The nurse unconsciously glanced at the empty bed across the bland, carbolic-smelling ward. When she glanced back her smiling face had changed to a more sober expression.

'He's another pilot, like you. Came in a few nights ago. They've sent him elsewhere.'

'But what's wrong with him? He was screaming blue murder last night,' Peter replied, shaking his head.

'Exhaustion, I think. Something like that anyway. There's a special hospital they go to. Not something *you* want to dwell on, my dear.'

Peter said nothing, the man's screaming had unnerved him. In his mind's eye he pictured him thrashing about beneath his blankets, waking the other patients. How a cockney voice at the end of the room shouted, *hoi mate, stick a sock in it.* And then the orderlies burst in, followed shortly after by a doctor holding a syringe. There was a struggle, muffled cries. And then the man seemed to float back into an all-consuming sleep. Peter shuddered at the thought.

Archie Cahill's smiling face appeared at the end of the bed.

'Hello beautiful,' he beamed.

'Lord, you RAF lot are saucy,' Inglis giggled.

'I wasn't talking to you, although you're not half bad too.' Cahill and the nurse erupted in laughter. Everyone in the otherwise quiet ward stared and it earned them an admonishment from the Ward Sister, who was supervising the dressing of a pressure ulcer two beds down. Peter rolled his eyes.

'Let me fetch you both a nice cuppa,' Inglis whispered before heading off.

'Well, that was some sortie, eh? You were damned lucky to

make it back. I looked over your aircraft before I drove here, and the thing looks like a bloody sieve.'

'I owe it all to the pilot who escorted me home. Any idea who it was?'

'Not really. Seems it was an aircraft from the Photographic Reconnaissance Unit. A new machine just off trials called a 'Mosquito'. Apparently, it's going to be quite the thing when it reaches Bomber Command.

'I dare say so, it had a hell of a turn of speed on it. I-.'

'How are you, Peter?'

'Alright, I suppose. I'll feel much better when I'm out of this place and back flying again.'

Archie cleared his throat and looked away.

'Is there something on your mind?'

'You won't be going back to flying. At least not yet.'

'What?'

'S.O.E. are furious about the loss of their man. Apparently he was some sort of talented wireless operator. They've demanded a thorough investigation; they believe you failed to follow standard operating procedures.'

'Well I don't recall seeing the recognition signal before I landed, but anyone could have overlooked that. It was the right landing field.'

Archie's eyebrows shot up, 'Christ Peter, you better save that for the investigation. Until it's completed, I'm afraid you better consider yourself removed from flying duties.'

'You're *grounding* me?'

'It's just procedure, Peter. You might try following it.'

Peter went to reply but stopped at seeing the nurse return with the tea. She laid the tray on the bed saying, 'Here we are. Oh, you're not leaving?'

'I'm sorry, Sister, duty calls,' Archie replied, 'Peter, I'll bring the car around to the front. Cheerio.' Archie drank off his tea and, flashing a winning smile, stalked off down the ward. The nurse watched him go with a vague, dreamy look in her eyes.

'Those RAF uniforms make me go weak at the knees,' Inglis said, eventually.

'It's not doing much for me at the moment.' Peter replied. He sipped his tea, stood, and took his sponge bag.

'You be careful, love.' Inglis smiled.

Peter departed the ward and entered a long, high-ceilinged corridor. He paid little attention to the few patients and medical staff he passed, absorbed in his own thoughts as he was. Thoroughly professional, Peter had never once been grounded and, though it might have been procedure, it was humiliating. He told himself he might just as easily have heeded the missing signal and earned a reprove for failing to deliver the agent.

'Excuse me, chum,' he said to someone barring his way, then realised with a shock it was Jumbo Sutherland.

'Hello Peter.'

'My god, it's you,' Peter said, studying Sutherland's face, which seemed paler and more pinched without the beard he'd sported in Greece. An uneasy feeling in his stomach told him this was no coincidence.

'How've you been keeping?'

'I'm bearing up. You've missed visiting hour, you know?'

'Actually, I came here to speak to you. In here.' Checking over his shoulder, Sutherland gripped his arm and opened the door next to him. He pulled Peter forcefully into a room that opened off the corridor. With the light on, Peter saw it was a medical storeroom. Scrubbed stretchers lined the wall opposite and bed pans were piled untidily in one corner.

'I need your help,' Sutherland said, closing the door firmly behind him. 'It concerns Eve. She's in trouble.'

'Eve? What sort of trouble?'

'The gravest kind. I sent her to France to investigate a spy ring, but I've since discovered that the Germans are playing us, and I need to get her out quickly.'

Peter's mind swam at this revelation. He attempted to think through the implications of what Sutherland had told him, eventually replying, 'I've just been grounded. How can I be of use to you now?

'I know, that's why I wanted to speak to you. I have no idea where to begin with planning an extraction, but we can start by narrowing down the places we can land. You can look through all the sortie records held by 1419 Flight; you know where all the in-use landing zones are. You must find out which is the emergency escape route used by Grapple.'

'Grapple?'

'Sound familiar to you?'

'It was on a Grapple sortie that I got this.' Peter pointed to his bandaged neck.

'So, you understand why I can't ask S.O.E. for this information then.'

'But those details are kept secure. I don't have access without breaking just about every rule in the book. If I'm found out, they'll do more than ground me; it's a court-martial offence.'

'Eve's life depends on it.'

Any further objections died in his throat. Peter set his jaw and asked, 'What do we do when we've got it?'

'We'll cross that bridge when we come to it. In the meantime, concentrate on learning the details of Grapple's escape route. I'll pull some strings to make sure you stay where you are. We don't want some damned fool getting ideas about posting you to a staff job,' Sutherland snorted.

'I'd better be going,' Peter said. 'Archie will be wondering what's happened to me.'

Peter hesitated momentarily, his hand on the doorknob.

'Did *you* arrange for me to go to Special Duties?'

Sutherland didn't reply, but instead removed his pipe from his jacket pocket and placed it between his teeth.

'I hope you've got a good plan, Sutherland.'

'Good luck m'boy, I'll be in touch. And Peter?'

Halfway out the door, Peter turned around in surprise.

'Yes?'

'Don't get caught.'

*

In a squalid little cafe down a back street behind the inner-harbour at Concarneau, Jean Morvan sipped his cognac and listened to the hushed whisper of his companion. The man had nothing to say that Morvan did not already know. A rumour of German troop movements from the Biscay coast, gossip about U-Boat crews' morale; the usual *merde*.

'The Germans visit prostitutes because they are well paid and because they are weeks at sea,' Morvan said patiently. 'Not because their morale is failing. I don't pay you to regurgitate this rubbish.'

'You hardly pay me at all,' the man grumbled.

'And I won't pay you again if you continue to waste my time.'

Morvan placed his empty glass on the table and reached into his pocket for some change. He stood to go.

'Wait. There is something else.'

Morvan made a sceptical face but sat down wearily at the table once more, looking pointedly at his watch.

'What? This better be good.'

'There was a raid, a few weeks ago now, on Brest.'

'So?'

'One of the bombers was shot down, but an airman survived. He's being hidden on a farm not too far from here. Is that worth anything to you?'

'Maybe. I'll have to check with *Le Renard*. I'll get back to you.'

'You know *Le Renard*?' He sounded impressed, as well he might be. The man was fast becoming a legend in the Resistance for his exploits against the Germans, and the French who worked for them.

'I know many people,' Jean Morvan replied pointedly. 'Both living and dead.' He stood once more, leaving the words hanging in the air, and swept out of the bar.

Chapter Ten

Stolcher clapped his hands together in glee as he heard the news. The gesture caused the few staff on duty to stare, so unexpected was this display of enthusiasm. He slammed the telephone receiver down and gazed around at the office staff. He wanted to shout that his field team had just bagged the lone agent he was fretting about, but then he remembered he had excluded them from this knowledge in the first place.

'I'm heading to Avenue Foch,' he said eventually. 'Where is the *ZINNMAN* dossier?'

'Here Herr Hauptsturmfuhrer.'

There was his leather attaché case. It went everywhere with him by force of habit; no self-respecting counter-intelligence agent would leave sensitive documents just lying around. And *ZINNMAN* wasn't merely sensitive, it was explosive. He'd seen enough of what was in that attaché case to know it could never fall into the hands of the British. The security of the Reich depended on it. Not for the first time, Stolcher told himself, he was playing with fire.

At Avenue Foch, he waved his identification at the sentry in the lobby and took the stairs at a run up to the private first-floor office. Guhr stood awkwardly outside, his heavy face beset by some unknown trouble.

'Well done, Guhr, well done. But what's this, hm? Something on your mind?'

'We got the girl, but she shot Alois. He didn't make it. And the Dubreys woman was killed in the crossfire.'

Stolcher sighed, 'It could have been much worse though, eh?'

Guhr blinked away disbelief, 'Well, Alois was due to marry-'

'Yes, yes. And most importantly,' Stolcher continued, 'You got the girl. Has she started singing yet?'

'No, she's upstairs. I was going to get Heinz and Dieter to work her over, they were close friends with Alois.'

'I want to see her first.'

'But you never visit on the first day of an interrogation.'

'This is different. This one arrived without my knowledge and I need to know how, and why.'

Stolcher launched the attaché case at Guhr and left him standing dumbly in the corridor to make the familiar ascent to the interrogation floor. He was feeling far more benevolent towards Guhr these past weeks, he realised as he climbed the stairs. Before, he had thought of him as a mere oaf, suited to interrogation work and nothing more. But now the man fulfilled a role approaching that of his deputy. He was almost warming to him.

Through the security door, he fought the urge to whistle to himself. Whatever risks he had run were now at an end, the girl would talk, and Operation BALDUR would be an enormous success. Even in the highly politicised environment of the R.H.S.A. there could be no denying the victory he was about to score over the British. It could only mean promotion for him personally, perhaps even an honour from *der Führer* himself; his heart skipped.

Regardless of what he'd achieved, Stolcher never let himself lose sight of his low birth and his early career in Weimar Germany. All his accomplishments up to this point had only permitted him to drag himself free from the morass of poverty, alcoholism, and illiteracy that had been his childhood. To come this far had taken more than a reasonable amount of sweat and tears, not to mention all the blood. Although that had mostly belonged to other people.

Ignoring the guard at the door, he straightened his tie and

turned into the opened cell, whereupon he stopped dead. Guhr failed to mention the girl was so pretty. It would be a crying shame, what he would have to do to her. Handcuffed to a chair in the middle of the room, she exuded a quiet hatred. His face relaxed into a sardonic smile.

'I see the British are so desperate for agents that they're sending their children now. Who are you?'

The girl stared mutely at the bare wall behind him.

'Fine, I'll introduce myself. My name is Hauptsturmfuhrer Erich Stolcher, and I work for the Reich security service,' Stolcher said in his best English. The girl looked bored.

'It will be easier for you in the long-run if you cooperate, you know. Your friends have. You were caught at a known S.O.E. safe house, with an illegal wireless, and you shot someone with a British weapon. Really, I ought to give you to my men to soften up. But I thought you'd see the hopelessness of your position now.'

She remained silent and indifferent. Stolcher's cheeks burned, recognising the girl's disdain for his questioning technique. He knew at this point he should bring in the heavies, he'd already broken his own rules by even being here. But a small part of him wanted this challenge, just for the thrill of it.

'Fine. Let me tell you what I plan to do with you, and then you can think about what I've said. First, I'll let a couple of my strongest men work you over for a day or so. They won't even ask you any questions, they'll knock you around just for fun. I'll come back to see you after that and we can talk about anything you want. But if you remain silent-,' Stolcher licked his lips unconsciously. 'Well, we have other ways of inducing you to talk. Don't forget, you're mine now and I can do whatever I want with you.'

The girl turned slowly to look at him. When her eyes met his, what he saw there robbed him of words. She was completely unafraid. His rage boiled over, and he fetched her a swift back-hander. The blow almost lifted her off the chair, but she quickly recovered and looked back at him with ill-disguised hatred. An ugly red welt crossed her pale cheek where his ring scored the flesh.

'You *made* me do that,' Stolcher yelled, spittle spraying from his mouth. His mind was spinning from the realisation that, somehow, he had not established his power in this interrogation. It was with a feeling of deep unease that he shouted for the guard's return. When he appeared, Stolcher noticed the man's tunic was unbuttoned. He wore a look of surprise on his face, accentuated by the lit cigarette that dangled from his lips. If he had expected the questioning to last much longer, then he was to be disappointed.

'Button your jacket up, you slob. Go fetch Guhr and tell him to take this bitch to Fresnes for the night, then bring her back in the morning.'

'Jawhol, Herr Hauptsturmfuhrer!'

'And you,' Stolcher whipped around to face the girl, 'You better have a think about just how much trouble you're in.'

*

The aircraft descended sharply as it crossed the coast so that it was low, very low, by the time it passed Charlie overhead. Shading his eyes from the bright sun, he recognised it as a Focke-Wulf 200 Condor. It was a long-range reconnaissance aircraft that patrolled far out into the Atlantic, preying on British shipping. But this one had reached too far by the looks of it. One of its engines was out and another trailed a thin wisp of grey smoke. Charlie pushed his broad-brimmed hat back on his head and leant against the side of the ditch he had been clearing. The Condor disappeared behind a tall wood on the far hills to the east. It was the only sign in these last few weeks that the war continued without him, and it cheered him to see.

'Good riddance you bastard,' he said to himself.

He strained to hear the resultant explosion, but none came. Instead, he heard Cecile approaching from the yard by her cheery whistle. He smiled to himself at hearing the tune.

'Charlie, I have something here for you,' she shouted, seeing his head and shoulders above the earth. He had quite forgotten that it was noon, so totally absorbed was he in his duties.

'Oh my,' Cecile said. 'You must have cleared the length of the field this morning. You are not famished?'

'Come to think of it, *mon cher*, I am,' Charlie replied, his stomach growling pleasantly at the thought of a meal.

Cecile produced a thick slab of cheese encompassed by a thin baguette, which she had wrapped in cloth. Charlie eyed it hungrily as she set it down alongside a couple of clay cups and a bottle.

'This is our own cider. We produce it from the orchards, but the Germans take almost all of it for themselves, along with three-quarters of our crops and our cheese.'

Charlie raised a cup to his lips, barely registering it was the first alcohol he had tasted in weeks. It was cool and refreshing and before he knew it, he had drained it. Cecile leaned over to refill it, but he placed his hand over the bowl.

'I mustn't, thank you.'

'Why not Charlie?'

'I used to drink heavily, to treat migraines. From an injury. D'you see? But the drinking got the better of me and it made me a person that I didn't like. I haven't touched a drop until now, and I think it better if I stay clear of the stuff. Just for the time being.'

'But of course. Do you still feel the pain?'

'You know, I can't say I do. It seems to have evaporated since I've been here.'

Cecile smiled and watched him devour his sandwich. He had

no idea what cheese it was, but it tasted deliciously creamy and salty; it was a perfect accompaniment to the cider.

'This is wonderful, thank you,' he beamed.

'What do you make of our cheese?'

'It's lovely, not unlike a ripe Brie. It stinks though, like old socks.'

Cecile burst out laughing, covering her mouth as she convulsed. Charlie grinned at the sight. When she eventually recovered Charlie asked her, 'How do you make a living if the Germans take most of your produce? Surely it makes farming impossible if you can't make a profit?'

'Well, they get three quarters of what we *declare*. Some of our produce is hidden from them, much of it in underground stores around the farm. We can sell it illegally and it helps us survive. The Germans pay us in their stupid worthless money, which is basically plunder. They are stripping France of all its resources to feed their fat, lazy Nazi wives in Germany.' Cecile spat in anger, her face suddenly flushed red.

This time Charlie laughed, great guffaws at the sight of her unusual hot temper.

'What? Why are you laughing?'

'I'm not laughing,' Charlie laughed.

'Stupid. This is no laughing matter,' Cecile said, a faint smile beginning at the edges of her mouth.

Soon they were both laughing like a pair of lunatics, so much so that Pascal was able to creep up on them unannounced. His ugly head appeared above the ditch and the sight was so instantly disagreeable to Charlie that he stopped laughing and stared up at the young man. Pascal shot Charlie his habitual look of dislike before speaking to Cecile in his rapid, whiny voice. Several weeks' immersion had not passed without some improvement in his French, and Charlie could pick out a few words. So, before Pascal turned and walked off, Charlie knew that whatever he had to say concerned Cecile's father and a visit of some kind.

'We have to go back to the house,' Cecile said.

Charlie threw his shovel out of the ditch and clambered out, noticing by a cool breeze about his midriff that M. Ropars' second-best trousers threatened to escape the belt holding them up. He had lost some weight during his sojourn in France.

'What's his problem?' Charlie jutted his chin at Pascal's back, 'Has he always got a face like a slapped arse?'

'Like a what?'

'He's a right ignorant prat.'

Cecile gave him an understanding look but said nothing. They walked in silence for a time before she replied, 'Pascal wants to marry me, and to inherit the farm. Papa treats him like a kind of a son, but only because he lost a son himself.'

'I'm so sorry, was it in the war?'

'No. He was a baby. It was a long time ago, and now they just have me.'

'Just?' Charlie rolled his eyes, 'You're better than any son.'

Cecile blushed and looked away, so Charlie went on, 'I take it that you don't feel the same about Pascal then?'

'He's an ignoramus. All he knows is what he's learned here. He never travelled further than Brest in his whole life, but he thinks he can lecture me on my duties as a woman. Pah.' Cecile gave an angry shrug.

'And what are they?'

'To cook for him, to clean-,' Cecile clapped her hand onto her fist in a gesture Charlie had never seen before, 'To bear him a child.' At Charlie's bemused look Cecile laughed again.

'He sounds like a bloody fascist-,'

'Shhh. Charlie, listen.' Cecile seized Charlie's arm and placed a finger against her lips.

Some way off in the distance, Charlie thought he could hear

the faintest sound of an engine approaching. A motorcycle engine.

'The Boches! Quick, follow me. *En avant.*'

Eve grabbed Charlie's hand and led him at a run away from the farmhouse, down the side of a fallow field and to the edge of a small wood. As they ran, Charlie noticed the way in which Cecile's simple cotton dress sat on her hips. Perhaps it was the cider, he pondered, but he had not been conscious that Cecile had a figure at all before now. His heart thumped wildly and threatened to beat out of his chest by the time they reached a stone wall. Behind it was an indentation in the ground. She dropped to her knees and frantically swept aside some foliage to reveal a few wooden boards covering a hidey-hole.

'Get in,' she ordered.

Charlie jumped into the hole, finding it much deeper than he expected and crammed with hessian sacks and clay jugs. Cecile's slender legs hung comically in the opening for a moment before she too dropped in after him, pulling across the boards and their concealment over her head and plunging them both into darkness.

The sound of the motorcycle grew clearer and louder as it approached the house. Charlie pictured it making the final turn onto the long, straight avenue that led up to the farm. The Ropars would see it by now and must know that Cecile had taken Charlie to hide.

He almost yelled out as something crawled across his fingers, but then he realised that Cecile had reached out to grasp his hand. He shook his head in the pitch black, but nevertheless squeezed back. If the Germans had really come for him, then a moment's affection from a beautiful young Frenchwoman was hardly a crime, he thought.

The motorcycle cut out and silence fell. Robbed of his sight, Charlie's other senses took over. The hiding place smelt strongly of barley and earth, and the sweet musk of Cecile's hair. He was unsure how much time passed before rustling grass foretold the approach of someone above. But then it stopped, and Charlie thought that the searcher must have passed by.

The cover to the hiding place was yanked away. It admitted the strong afternoon sun causing Charlie to shield his eyes. He felt Cecile grip his other hand tighter still. Then M.Ropars cleared his throat and said, 'Uh Charlie, you must come with me. You have a visitor.'

*

Fresnes prison was a stark brick pile constructed towards the beginning of the Third Republic. Its towering walls and lofty cell blocks rendered escape impossible for even the most determined inmate. An impression that Eve formed almost immediately upon arrival and even before she was marched to the damp, fetid cell. The mute jailor removed her cuffs and shoved her in, slamming the heavy iron door behind her. A thin beam of light shone through the single window high up at the end of the room, through which several iron bars could be seen.

Other than a filthy straw-filled mattress on the concrete, the only other features of the space were a necessary pail and a thick pipe running across the ceiling. From its width, it appeared that the pipe travelled across several other cells on this side of the block before going elsewhere. Occasionally, it burbled. Eve did not need to inspect the window to know that it offered no viable exit. She leaned back against the wall and tried to take stock of her situation.

She felt angry with herself for how easily she'd walked into the trap at the safe house. Lise Dubreys might have paid for her duplicity with her life, but Eve raged at the thought of how many other agents had been betrayed in this manner. If she still had possession of her coat, she would have taken her cyanide ampule by now.

Although she had put on a good show for her interrogator, the truth was that she was tired, and she was beginning to feel a little afraid. Not of dying though. That barely registered for her. Eve was afraid of letting herself down by giving in to the torture that she knew would come in the morning. She was experienced enough in intelligence work to know that everyone had a breaking point. Everyone gave up in the end. Even before she had reached the end of this train of thought, she had decided that she had one opportunity to escape. It would come tomorrow in the interval between leaving Fresnes and arriving at Avenue Foch. She would take it, and perhaps die in the act. This was still better than any of the other alternatives.

Eve tried to visualise how she would go about her attempt. But was interrupted by the opening of a slot at ground-level in the iron door. A tin plate slid through the hole and came to a rest near her feet. On it was a pale, glutinous mass of something unappetising. Some form of stew that was long on pulses and not much else, she guessed. She turned her head away from it. A nagging echo in her mind told her that she needed to eat and sleep, regardless of how she felt. Exhausted people wore down faster under interrogation. But something that was neither tiredness nor hunger intruded upon her anxious mind. It was a constant sound, only just audible. She strained to listen and realised that it was tapping.

The pipe did not burble at random. Someone was quietly and rhythmically tapping it from another cell and the echo could be heard all along its length. The longer Eve listened, the more she became convinced there was a pattern in the signal. It was not Morse, there were too many beats to each section; it could only be a melody. She hummed the beats, and as she did so, the words came to her as if from a childhood memory.

Oranges and Lemons,

Say the bells of St. Clement's,

Eve searched about for something to tap with and her eyes fell upon the plate. She flicked the slop off it and found that, by standing on her tiptoes, she could just about reach the pipe. She waited for the tapping to die away and replied.

You owe me five farthings,

Say the bells of St. Martin's,

She listened for a reply. Silence.

'Oh, please say something. Don't lose your tongue now,' she begged.

The tapping resumed, but now it was rushed and clearly in the pattern of dots and dashes that could only be Morse. It was a message, 'Who are you?'

Eve thought for a moment. There was a possibility this was an elaborate attempt to ensnare her. The British too eavesdropped on their prisoners, it was a valuable and subtle method of gathering intelligence. But her interrogator had said that 'her friends' had cooperated, which meant that the other Grapple agents might be at Fresnes too. Of course, an interrogator would say anything to add to an intelligence agent's discomfort. Eve decided she was already too compromised by her capture to worry about the risk of worsening the situation now.

She tapped back, 'I'm with Grapple. Who are you?'

Again, silence followed. If she was conversing with a Grapple agent, they might too question whether they were being played by the Germans. Perhaps, she told herself, she would hear nothing more from the other end of the pipe.

The tapping resumed, slowly and deliberately now, like someone coming to the end of a portentous confession. Eve followed it, word by painstaking word.

'I am Plainfare.'

Chapter Eleven

Missing, believed killed. Peter could hardly understand the words spoken to him by Johnny Corbett. On his first sortie too, it was senseless. It had never been Peter's intention for this to happen, he just wanted Charlie to avoid a lengthy and embarrassing trial. The aircraft had failed to return from a bombing mission in France, there was always some hope that a few had got out.

'Stranger things have happened,' Corbett said, unconvincingly.

'Thank you for calling,' Peter had replied.

Charlie's loss did not change Peter's decision to commit treason, it accelerated it. No-one, Peter told himself, sets out to wilfully break the rules. And yet rules get broken. Sometimes through expedience or incompetence, or because it is easier to proliferate rules than it is to understand their effect on an organisation. Occasionally, such as in this case, the rules must be broken out of necessity.

Peter surmounted this moral hurdle in his mind whilst working on 1419 Flight, not as a pilot but as a non-flying officer. It was a perspective that Peter was unaccustomed to and he bitterly disliked it. Archie had tried to oust him, of course, justifying it as bad luck having a grounded flier about with an investigation underway. But whatever strings Sutherland had pulled worked a treat, the day after their meeting a signal arrived appointing Peter as the unit's Adjutant. When he saw that he couldn't dispose of Peter in the conventional way, Archie adopted a more subtle approach: he tried to drown him in bullshit.

Some of this was naturally Peter's job. The Adjutant handled all the administration for the Flight and was usually up to the elbows in signals, letters, returns, and registers of this and that. But Archie sent everything Peter's way, so he had to deal with engineering and supply problems too. When Peter solved one of these thorny problems, another two seemed to pop up to replace it. In this manner, the weeks flew by.

He thought back to his friend Brian Potterne, who had been the Adjutant on his previous squadron, and wondered how he'd managed it all without losing his mind. 'Potty' had airmen to assist him with the burden, whereas Peter had only the ancient Corporal MacGill under his command, and MacGill wasn't really an assistant. MacGill's job was to be guardian of the Task Plans Cell, a repository of information about previous missions flown by 1419 Flight. It contained all the details of passengers dropped off or recovered, and airstrips used for Special Duties flying since 1940. If Peter was to discover which secret landing strip was used as the emergency by Grapple, then he needed unfettered access to those files. Even when he had the information he required, there was the small matter of the rescue itself.

Peter dismissed the negative thoughts crowding his mind. He needed to accomplish the first part of the task before he worried about the other. The first obstacle was Archie Cahill. Like most senior RAF officers, Cahill was devoted to his work. When flying operations were on, Cahill often worked a twenty-hour day, only returning to the Mess for breakfast and a nap before the next evening's orders arrived. This moon period still had another 10 days to run on it, so there was no question of waiting until the next lunar phase. Once he had avoided Cahill, he still had to deal with MacGill who was always present in the Task Plans Cell when it was open and always locked it when he left. That was going to be far trickier.

The more Peter wracked his brains for an answer to his puzzle, the less it seemed to be in reach. He stood, grabbed his cigarettes and decided to take a walk in the hope inspiration would come. He passed Cahill's office, who was head-down scribbling something at his desk, and left the building.

A gentle summer sun caressed his face as he stepped out onto the dispersal, it was followed by the whiff of aviation fuel. He opted to walk away from the airfield and towards the concrete pads the Lysanders stood on. His own aircraft wasn't here, the damage it had sustained was too great for the engineers to deal with on the flight line. So, his Lizzie was over in one of the large hangars on Tangmere's main site where more extensive repairs could be carried out. Nevertheless, three Lysanders were present in differing states of readiness, the nearest had its engine panels stripped away for routine servicing. A couple of shirtless engineers worked on it with their black overalls tied around their waists, whilst their sergeant sat under the shade of the wing reading a paper.

'Alright sergeant? Oh, please don't get up, it's too hot for that.'

'Good mornin' sir,' the sergeant beamed. Peter didn't recognise him, but it was clear that the man wished to be remembered. And then the penny dropped.

'You were here when I brought my aircraft back, weren't you?'

'That's right, sir, I helped tow your kite back over to the dispersal afterwards. She was fair shot up and all. That was some flying you must've done to get her back 'ome. Shame about your passenger.'

'Yes,' Peter replied thoughtfully, 'It was. Was the aircraft much beaten about?'

'Nothing they can't fix in the workshop. Those old Lysanders are child's play compared to some of the aircraft I've worked on. Anyway, I expect she'll be back after an air test. And that's planned for Friday afternoon.'

Friday afternoon gave him 48 hours to work out where Grapple's emergency landing field was. As he turned this new information over in his mind, an awkward silence fell between the two of them. Peter tried hopelessly to find words of conversation until he spied the paper crammed in the sergeant's armpit.

'Anything in today's news?'

'Not much. A few stories about the invasion of the U.S.S.R.'

'Some good news, at last. Are they making much headway?'

'The Germans? Seems so. I was just doing the crossword though, sir. You any good with words?'

'I get by. Why don't you try me?'

The sergeant opened the paper to the section near the back and ran his hand down the grid to where an unfilled line defied his vocabulary.

'8 letters. Begins with 'L' and ends in 'E'.'

'What's the clue?'

'A medicine that relaxes.'

Peter thought for a moment. It felt like the answer was just at the end of his fingertips.

'I've got it,' he exclaimed. 'It's *laxative.*'

The sergeant chuckled and, removing a stubby pencil tucked behind his ear, he wrote the word in.

'What a shit clue,' he grinned, but seeing Peter's unmoved face he coughed and added, 'Fits like a glove, thank you for your help sir.'

But Peter's mind was no longer on crosswords, for inspiration had just struck. He knew exactly how he was going to fix Corporal MacGill.

*

The man sat at the kitchen table did not look like a resistor, although Charlie admitted to himself he had no clear idea what a member of the Resistance should look like. His round, almost cabbage-like, head sat on thin, drooping shoulders. He nursed a glass of brandy and surveyed Charlie quietly with the dark, expressionless eyes of a predator. When he spoke, his voice was so heavily accented that it was hard to follow him.

'You say you were shot down two weeks ago, during a bombing raid on Brest?'

'Yes, that's about right.'

'And your squadron? I have no record of anyone with your name posted as missing.'

'I was only with 75 Squadron for a matter of hours before that raid,' Charlie replied with a faint tone of exasperation. 'The administration might not have caught up from my previous unit.'

'Well, 75 Squadron didn't lose any aircraft either. You're a lying bastard, Kendrick. Who do you work for, Gestapo eh?'

'What?' Charlie looked about for support but saw none. The Ropars had been collectively dismissed to another room whilst this interview took place. He tried again.

'Look, this is daft. All my documentation and my uniform were burnt so it couldn't compromise us. I've been pretending to be a farm labourer. Do I sound like a kraut to you?'

'If you *sounded* like a kraut we wouldn't be speaking now,' his interrogator said, pulling a snub-nosed pistol from his jacket and pointing it at Charlie's heart. 'Tell me who you work for.'

'Jesus Christ, what's wrong with you? I told you that I'm Flight Lieutenant Charlie Kendrick, serving with 75 Squadron. I shouldn't even be here.'

'Why not?'

'I was busted to operations for hitting my boss.'

The Frenchman looked hard at Charlie for a moment, then his face creased up and he let out an enormous booming laugh. A wave of relief washed over Charlie as the pistol was placed on the table. Red-faced and doubled up, the inquisitor finally managed to compose himself enough to reply, 'No Bosche could ever dream of treating his superior like that, you must be legitimate.'

He poured himself another glass of brandy and beckoned M. and Mme. Ropars back into the room from the doorway where they had been eavesdropping. Mme. Ropars explained with a shrug of embarrassment that they 'heard laughter and wanted to check that all was *d'accord*'.

'Who are you?'

'My name is Victor Resonet, but they also call me *Le Renard*. I work for the Resistance, organising things.'

'But what do you organise?'

'Things. Like I said.' Resonet made a non-committal face and sipped his liquor.

'You're here to get me out? You know of an escape line?'

'In time, yes.'

'In time?'

'Yes.'

'I'm sorry but you're being very vague. Are you here to help me or not?'

'I will help you get back to England. But first I need your help with something.'

'Me? What use could I possibly be to you?'

'A friend of mine has encountered some troubles with the Germans and needs a hand to get home too. Their situation is not unlike yours, no?'

'A rescue attempt? Look here Victor, I'm a bloody navigator in the RAF, not some-' Charlie struggled to find an appropriate term, '-brigand. I barely even know how to handle a weapon.'

'I can teach you, there is time.'

Charlie glanced over to Cecile who had entered behind her parents and was helping her mother attend to the cooking pot.

Both pretended not to listen. He lowered his voice, 'I just don't think that now is a wise time to go running around occupied France. I've no uniform or papers and if I get caught, they'll shoot me.'

'If you get caught, they'll shoot you anyway. No, *mon frère*,' Victor looked from Charlie to Cecile, who looked away the moment their eyes met, and back again. 'I think I understand your reluctance to leave Kerluen.' A look of quiet intelligence appeared on Victor's face, Charlie knew he had been smoked as both a coward and a womaniser. He wanted to tell him that he'd got it all wrong, that Charlie never intended to sit out the war here. But he craved a rest; he needed the time to get better. Time that the RAF had not granted him. He opened his mouth, but the words died away unsaid. It struck Charlie that anything short of an unequivocal commitment to canter away in pursuit of Victor's damned fool friend would sound mean and unworthy. Certainly, to a patriot like Victor who no doubt ran unimaginable risks for his cause.

Victor looked away, probably keen to avoid the embarrassment altogether. Seeing it, Mme. Ropars asked, 'Will you stay for dinner, it is almost done.'

'*Non merci*.' Victor drained his glass and with a sideways look at Charlie said, 'Your kindness has been too great already.'

Charlie felt wretched at Victor's display of silent disappointment, yet he was enough of a man to stand and offer his hand to him. With eyebrows raised, Victor took it and said in a low voice, 'If you change your mind, there is a bistro in Rennes. It is a rendezvous for our group on Rue Gurvand, near the Place de la Gare. Ask for Francois. It is never too late, Charlie.' He kissed Mme. Ropars on each cheek, embraced M. Ropars, and left silently through the kitchen door.

The Ropars said nothing as the sound of Victor's motorcycle faded away in the distance, but Charlie sensed they too knew what had happened. They ignored it, choosing to concentrate on the preparation of dinner. He left the house without a word and walked back towards the fields, his mind spinning. An iron-bottomed feeling of depression spread over him as he considered how wretched he was. Even his friend, Peter, had tired of him eventually.

As he reached the thicket of trees that screened the house from its nearest field, he heard rapid footsteps through the grass behind him. Turning, he saw Cecile sprinting at him full pelt, her golden hair streamed out behind her. He caught her in his arms and saw that her cheeks glistened with tears. She gave him one quivering, distressed look and buried her head in his chest.

'My dear,' he said. 'Whatever is the matter?'

'Oh Charlie, I thought you would go with Victor; I thought you were leaving me.'

*

By the low growl of a running truck engine beyond the gate, Eve knew her time was up. Though she did not normally feel fear or anxiety, both those emotions hovered close to the surface as the prison's heavy iron gates yawned open to admit the canvas-backed Opel Blitz. It swung around in the courtyard until it faced back the way it had come, and a soldier climbed out of the cab to lower the tailgate. A second German jumped down, followed by a giant of a man wearing the dark green leather overcoat common to members of the Gestapo. She'd not seen him before now, but it was clear from his size that he would be a very formidable opponent indeed.

A tug at her wrists reminded her of the presence of a prison warder, now removing her cuffs with practiced speed. As he bent towards her, she caught the scent of stale body odour and fetid breath. Then her hands were free, but the Germans stood around her like crows surveying an earthworm. The giant addressed the warder in halting French, telling him to fetch any paperwork and to be quick about it. One of the soldiers produced a chain linked by a pair of metal T-pieces, it was a restraint method that Eve had seen before. Some called it a 'come-along' cuff, since it relied on not a lock, like conventional handcuffs, but instead the guard's grip on the T-pieces to control the prisoner. With the chain looped about her wrist, the soldier could bring convincing pressure to bear with this method, as he demonstrated now by forcing her arm up painfully behind her back.

A white-hot pain shot up her shoulder causing Eve to cry out and swear, but the soldier just laughed and said something to his mate who leered grotesquely at her. He leaned down and removed her shoes one at a time, before throwing them away. Clearly, he thought this would make it harder for Eve to get away. She was led to the truck by the wrist and dragged forcefully up the tailgate where she was shoved into a sitting position near the back. The tall German followed shortly after. Sitting opposite her on the wooden bench his head nearly touched the canvas roof. The tailgate slammed shut and the Opel Blitz lurched off, turning right out of the high gateway and heading north.

She knew Paris and she knew the shortest route the driver could take to Avenue Foch. He would most likely enter the city through the Porte D'Orleans and pass to the west of Montparnasse, crossing the Seine on the Pont de Bir-Hakeim. With every mile they travelled, her opportunity to escape diminished as German military and security units were concentrated about the centre of Paris. If she was to be successful, if she was to carry home the vital information that she'd gained from Plainfare last night, then she must make a move now. In the remaining moments before they entered the city.

She glanced about her, at the big German opposite who

averted his gaze and at the soldier alongside who stared into the middle distance, alone in his thoughts. This single glance was enough to assure her that there were no other options, other than the plan that was gestating in her head. She quietly shifted her backside forward on the bench seat until it rested just on the edge. Then she waited. She waited for the right moment to come, knowing that when it did, she would have only seconds to make her escape. The truck slowed as some unseen obstruction in front halted the traffic.

Quick as a flash, Eve brought her leg up and launched her foot hard until it connected with the giant's crotch. He cried out in pain and doubled over. Her German guard leapt up in surprise at the unexpected sight and let go of the cuff, as Eve predicted he would. Her free hand found the soldier's bayonet and, in one fluid movement, she pulled it from its frog and plunged it deep into his belly. Choking and gasping he collapsed into the truck bed as his blood soaked through his field grey uniform. A fierce pain in her lower back sent her sprawling over the dying German and she turned to see the huge Gestapo man had recovered sufficiently to knock her down. The force was like being kicked by a mule, but Eve had no time to take stock of her injury as the red-faced German stood ready to deal the coup de grâce.

The end of the cuff was in her hand and she threw it at her attacker's head. He saw it coming and deflected it with one meaty forearm before leaning down to grab Eve about the throat. She felt his iron grip about her windpipe, squeezing hard. She couldn't breathe and felt a darkness appearing at the edge of her vision. How could it possibly end like this, she asked herself as her hands probed around for some weapon to fight for her life. She found it just before the darkness became total, the bayonet handle. With all her remaining strength, she jerked it free from the soldier's body and swung it around to bury it in the giant's side. She pulled the blade out and buried it again and again. Each time, the man howled in pain and his grip weakened.

If the German knew his end had come, he did not show it and continued to try to lash out at Eve who crawled to the back of the truck. On his knees he felt around for the blade stuck fast in his side, a high-pitched mewing drawn from his lips. Eve's vision cleared as the blood returned to her head. She pulled herself to her feet and stepped around the kneeling man, who watched her go almost wordlessly. The Opel Blitz drove off as Eve dropped to the road, her clothes stained with the blood of the two dying men. A few onlookers paused in the street at the grisly scene.

The passenger door of a goods truck parked on the opposite side of the road opened and its driver beckoned to her. Any blood-soaked woman leaping from a German truck in broad daylight could still be sure of succour from some quarters of the French population and Eve took the offer without a second thought. In the cab, the driver motioned for her to lay in the footwell and pulled a thick tarpaulin across her that smelt of coal and mildew. But none of that mattered, because Eve had escaped. She was free.

Chapter Twelve

The kettle whistled urgently, sending a cloud of steam into the air. Grasping it with a folded cloth, Peter poured the steaming contents into an aluminium pot along with a slack handful of tea leaves and let it stew. He wanted the tea to stew because he needed to conceal the taste of the castor oil he was about to stir into it. The Station Medical Officer had recommended it for the constipation Peter had falsely claimed to be suffering with. The doctor had even gone so far as to find a small bottle for Peter, cautioning him to use only a teaspoonful or rue the consequences. But when he'd poured the tea, he added two teaspoonfuls of oil and a drop more for good measure. Then he topped it up with a generous helping of sugar.

Corporal MacGill beamed when the mug arrived at his desk, so rarely was he the recipient of such a kind gesture. Peter was in no mood to talk and, after the usual pleasantries about the weather, he retired to his office to await the outcome. From his desk he could not see directly into MacGill's room, but an angled mirror positioned atop a bookcase gave him a view of the man's head through a row of internal panes. He was writing and stopped occasionally to sip his brew.

'What-ho, Peter,' said Colin, his head appearing around the doorframe. 'This is where they've put you now. Blimey, it's a pokey little dungeon isn't it?'

Peter tried to steal a glance at the mirror, but Colin had entered the room now and blocked it from view.

'It's alright for what I need,' Peter replied testily.

'Look, I can touch both walls if I stretch my arms out. Was this a cleaning cupboard before?'

Peter couldn't resist a smile at Colin's stupid pose, 'I suppose you've popped in for something more important than that Jesus Christ impression? I'm choked with 'adjutantly' business.'

'Well I did rather want to talk to you about that. You were missed last night at the cottage, you know.'

'I had no idea there was a party on.'

'It was impromptu. I managed to get into a little field near Troyes on my second attempt and Slim hauled back a couple of Frenchmen who'd been on the run for a week. They brought champagne with them.'

'Good-oh.'

'Look, I know Archie has been giving you the stiff arm, but he's in a difficult position. He's got S.O.E. yelling at him on one hand and Bomber Command trying to poach his crews for missions on the other. As far as the rest of us go, nothing's changed. You'd see that if you weren't playing the mysterious loner. Pimpernel is a callsign, not a nickname.'

'I'm- I'm fine. Once this investigation is done, I'll be back to my old self,' Peter lied.

'That's the spirit,' Colin replied. Just then, Archie came bustling down the corridor. Putting his hat on as he passed, he grunted something intelligible at them and was gone. The outer door slammed. Peter glanced at his watch, which told him it was just gone 8.30 am.

'I presume Archie was at the party last night?'

'I'll say. He was shit-faced well before midnight.'

'So I see. Well, I better make a start on these-'

What Peter was going to start on was something Colin would never find out, because they were interrupted by the screech of a chair being pushed forcefully away from a desk. Corporal MacGill groaned loudly and uttered the words, 'Jesus and the saints.'

'Careful with that language, Corporal,' Peter called with mock sincerity as he raced past on his way to the toilets.

'What's got into him?'

'Eh? Oh,' Peter shrugged, 'Powdered eggs I'll warrant.'

Peter eyed the vacated office hungrily. His gaze returned to Colin who rolled his eyes and said, 'Well it looks like you've enough on your hands here. I'm heading off to the Mess for forty winks. Cheerio.'

Peter waited until the outside door slammed shut once more and then leapt from his office into the Task Plans Cell. He looked wildly about for MacGill's key and found it under a stack of maps. The key opened the metal filing cabinet in which details of all the previous sorties flown by 1419 Flight were contained. The top drawer was empty, the second only half full. Files were crammed inside in alphabetical order according to the mission name. AUTOGIRO was the first and it ran as far back as MUSICIAN. It was this drawer then, he told himself. GRAPPLE was about a third of the way in and took up about the same amount of space. Flicking through the files he passed his own mission, #9, and stopped when his fingers fell on a packet marked 'Emergency Fields and Special Instructions'.

Checking that MacGill had not returned, Peter pulled the file out just as the building's front door slammed again. Peter kicked the drawer shut, slid the file under the maps and eased himself into MacGill's chair just as Archie returned with a face like thunder. He did a double take and then retraced his steps into the office.

'What the blazes are you doing in here? Where's Corporal MacGill?'

'He had to step out, sir. Stomach complaint. I'm just minding the shop until he returns.'

'Right,' Archie replied, his face a mask of suspicion. 'I just popped back for my briefcase. But since I'm here now, I might as well take those post sortie reports from last night. The ones on that desk.'

'Where?'

'There, under your elbow.'

Peter glanced down at the stack of maps under which he'd concealed the intelligence he intended to steal. His heart raced as he tried to think of an excuse for why he had the file. The moment he lifted the maps it would be quite clear to Archie what he was about, and that would be a pretty thing to try to explain.

It was an act of provenance that Corporal MacGill appeared when he did, white-faced and sweating, because it distracted Archie just long enough for Peter to slide the pile towards him. The file dropped unseen into his lap, and he handed the maps over to Archie who took them without a second glance. Poor MacGill had not the chance to even enter the office before his body was wracked by another attack and went flying out of the building again, holding his stomach.

'Jesus,' Archie said with a shake of the head. 'That's why you don't order fish on a Monday.'

'Quite.'

'I'm heading off. Sure you're alright to mind the shop?'

'I'll be fine,' Peter replied, trying to conceal the immense relief flooding through him.

Back in his broom cupboard, Peter shoved the door shut and opened the file. Grapple's air landing officer had reconnoitred several fields suitable to land a Lysander on and most of them had an accompanying aerial photograph taken by the Photo Reconnaissance Unit. On the back of each was the latitude and longitude and a three-digit code that acted as the unique identifier.

The emergency landing ground for Grapple was near a village called Chambois-le-Fue. It was a long field, about 500 yards by the look of it, bordering the Foret de Breteuil. The village was reasonably small, a single church and perhaps a few hundred residents. He traced his finger between the landing ground and Paris and found it to be something like 50 miles from the edge of the city; a tough distance to cover in a day with the Germans in pursuit. With a start, he realised the field was only a matter of miles from a major Luftwaffe base at Evreux. There were fighters there, and quite possibly night fighters too. Peter clicked his tongue, that was too bad.

A knock at his door startled him and he pulled the photo and landing ground details from the file and crammed them inside his tunic. Then he closed the file and said, in a nonchalant voice, 'Come in.'

MacGill stood in the doorway, looking incredibly sorry for himself.

'Hello, Corporal. I locked up your office when I thought you'd be gone for some time.'

'Thank you, much obliged sir. Just a funny turn but I think everything is ship-shape and Bristol fashion now.'

'That's excellent news, oh,' Peter grabbed the file from his desk and handed it to MacGill. 'Squadron Leader Cahill wanted me to give you this. He said it needs to be locked away.' MacGill took the file without the question. So eager was he to resume his lonely vigil that he didn't ask how Cahill came to have it in the first place, or why Peter was handing it back without an accompanying issue slip.

With the door closed, Peter picked up the telephone receiver and asked for the number that Sutherland had given him at the hospital. As he waited for the connection, he reflected that the things he'd done for Sutherland so far were enough to have him cashiered, if not sent to prison. It would all pale in comparison to what came next, however.

'Sutherland.'

'It's me,' said Peter.

'You've got the information I asked for?'

'Yes. When are we going?'

'Tonight.'

'What? Really?'

'You've got plans for the weekend?'

'No,' Peter replied hastily. 'I just thought it would take time to pull a plan together.'

'Time is exactly what we don't have. I've just had a signal from Eve, she's on her way to the rendezvous. I've arranged for a trusted fixer to meet us at your landing ground.'

'Ok. But I'll need your help with this next bit.'

'Fine. What do you need me to do?'

'Help me steal an aeroplane.'

Sutherland, whose cold, impersonal tone Peter found somewhat intimidating, laughed out loud at this. It was an odd, gravelly croak that sounded not unlike he was having breathing difficulties. When he stopped there was a short pause before he asked, 'My dear boy, you don't think this is the first time I've pinched one of the King's aircraft, do you?'

*

The light was failing quickly, Charlie realised as he stacked straw in the stone barn. Kerluen boasted few animals, but the straw would be essential for the coming winter, both for the Ropars' stock as well as that of their neighbours. M. Ropars had been clear about that when he'd asked Charlie to order the barn after the harvest. It was hard, hot work and the sweat poured off him and soaked his loose-fitting shirt down to the waist. When he heard the wooden doors creak behind him, he hoped it was Cecile with something refreshing, but instead it was M. Ropars carrying a clay jug.

'Charlie,' he called. 'Charlie, you can stop now. This is fine work.'

'Thank you. Is that cider you have there?'

M. Ropars sat and proffered a cup, which Charlie accepted

gratefully. He glugged down several mouthfuls before he felt the farmer's gaze on him and stopped self-consciously.

'You know, this is difficult for me to say. As…as a father. But I can see the way Cecile looks at you. Don't try to deny it, Charlie. I too am a man, eh?'

'Sir, I can assure you that nothing untoward has happened between us. I've been…,' Charlie struggled for the right words. 'I mean, which is to say, her virtue is complete.' Charlie winced at that statement and longed for the ground to swallow him up whole.

'But of course,' M. Ropars laughed and then he too slugged the cider. Wiping his mouth, he fixed Charlie with a bemused look.

'I don't mean to say that your daughter is not pretty. She is. Just that I would never countenance taking liberties when you've been so kind to me.'

'I don't worry about Cecile; she can handle herself. But I worry about you and I worry about her heart.'

'I don't follow you.'

'She is an innocent girl. I know that Victor offered you a route home and that you declined his offer.'

'He wanted me to take part in some espionage work and-'

'*Oui*. But you said no, and I think you did so because you're in love with Cecile. No, let me speak. But you have to ask yourself, what kind of life can you promise her, or yourself for that matter? One day the Bosches will be defeated and the war will be over, and then questions will be asked about Charlie Kendrick. Where is he? What was he doing all this time? Your honour as a man will be gone. Pffft.' M. Ropars made the image of an explosion with his hands.

'I'll get back eventually, with or without the help of the Resistance. I just need more time to…to-'

'There is no more time, Charlie. here is only now, this

moment. And if you stay here, Cecile will only go on falling for you. And when you eventually do leave, she will spend her time worrying about whether you got home alive or not. Every day, worry will consume a part of her until, should you one day return here to a free-France, she will be entirely changed from the carefree girl you know now. She will be hardened and resentful at the wait and heartbreak you put her through. I tell you, the best thing you can do is take Victor's offer. Go now, before it's too late.'

Charlie said nothing but looked miserably at the half-empty jug in M. Ropar's hands.

'You're right,' he said finally. 'But I have to say goodbye to Cecile first.'

'If you must, Charlie. I'll pack you some things for the journey, it's quite a way to travel to Rennes.'

'Thank you.'

'In the short time you've been here, I've come to think of you like a son. This parting injures us all.'

Charlie took M. Ropars' hand and felt the old man's firm embrace. He stood wordlessly and left the barn, knowing that at this hour Cecile would be feeding the pigs in the far field. The walk was a blessing because it gave him time to compose himself and rehearse what he was going to say. A stiff evening breeze set in and, for that reason, Cecile only noticed him when he was practically beside her.

'Idiot. You made me jump. I thought it was a Bosche come to search the farm. What's wrong? You look so serious, Charlie.'

Cecile had emptied two pails of food scraps onto the ground inside the field and the pigs were lumbering over from their sunbathing spots to eat.

'There's no easy way to say this, my dear.'

'*Mais non*. Please Charlie, don't say that you're going with Victor. It's so dangerous.'

'Cecile-'

She turned from him and shoved his arm away. Her face was flushed red and her eyes filled.

'Why do you want to rush back to your goddamned war so soon. 'Aven't you seen enough killing?'

'We both know that it's my duty to escape. As much as I would love to see the war out here with you, it's impossible. This is my only way home. I *have* to go.'

Cecile opened her mouth to reply, but closed it again. She shot Charlie a wounded look, which would normally have caused him to laugh, under any other circumstances.

'Look, my mind's made up. I've really just come to say goodbye. Let's not part like this?'

'Go then. *Filer.*' Cecile crossed her arms.

'I'll be thinking of you always, Cecile.'

He turned to go, then felt her hand on his arm as she pulled him back. And then her lips were against his and he tasted her warm, salty tears in his mouth.

'Oh, Charlie.'

The yell from behind was barely audible, but he heard it all the same. Turning around, Pascal advanced upon him angrily with a shovel in his hand.

'Bastard,' he shouted. 'You keep your filthy dog paws off her. She's mine.'

'I don't belong to you or anyone,' Cecile shouted.

'Look,' Charlie said as he stepped between them, 'I think you ought to take a walk to cool off, chum.'

Pascal's fist landed squarely on the side of his head. Pain exploded in his temple and things went black. When he recovered consciousness, he found himself on all fours with Cecile screaming as Pascal's foot connected with his stomach. He rolled on the floor and doubled up to protect himself from whatever was coming next.

'You can't come here and take things that don't belong to you,' Pascal spat.

'Pascal please-,'

'Shut it, bitch. I'm telling the Germans about your little secret here and I might just forget you were involved, if you're lucky.'

Dazed, Charlie shook his head to recover his wits. His head throbbed and the flesh around his eye socket felt raw and swollen. Pascal might have looked like an eight stone weakling, but he fought dirty. He looked up at the Frenchman who was bending over to pick up the shovel. He needed to even the odds, and quick. Pascal might be handy, he consoled himself, but he never went to public school.

Pascal towered over Charlie with his shovel, poised to land a killer blow, when Charlie reached up and gripped his testicles like he was squeezing a tube of toothpaste. The effect was instantaneous. Pascal howled and dropped the shovel, he sagged to the ground where he writhed about in anguish. Charlie climbed to his feet and brushed dirt off his shoulders and arms. He was at a loss for what to do with him. There was no way he could be trusted with the Ropars after the threat he'd just made. He was still turning it over in his mind when the shovel scythed past him like a battle axe and slammed onto Pascal's head.

'Good Lord. What are you doing?'

'I'm giving this traitor his due,' Cecile replied, an unusual look of quiet anger on her face as she lifted the shovel again.

'Don't hit him again, you'll-'

The shovel dropped again with a sickening crunch. Pascal stopped moving.

'I don't think he's breathing, Charlie.'

'I shouldn't think so after that blow. Are you alright?'

'*Oui*. But you must go. Now.'

'But. But what about this?'

Charlie gestured to Pascal's sprawled body.

'I'll take care of it. Go.'

He pulled her to him and kissed her. One long, heartfelt embrace and then he tore himself away. There was no time to loop back to the house now to collect supplies, he needed to cover ground. Soon he was running down a dark country lane with only the light of the moon to show him the way. Running to make a rendezvous for which he was already late.

*

Stolcher knew Guhr was dead even before he'd set eyes on the interior of the Opel Blitz. He knew by the shouting in the courtyard and the calls for a doctor, that something was amiss. He did not need to see the faces of the disconsolate soldiers stood alongside the truck, nor the dark blood that dripped sickeningly onto the dry cobblestones when the tailgate was lowered.

Guhr's loss was one thing, he knew he would surmount it because he'd always viewed people as essentially replaceable. What stirred his emotions the most was how he had underestimated the prisoner. He had held her in the palm of his hand and cast her away. Both men in the back had been overpowered by a slip of a girl, that much was obvious. It was only a matter of deduction that they had both died from wounds inflicted by a single weapon, a bayonet lodged in Guhr's side.

'Herr Hauptsturmfuhrer-' A uniformed major began.

'Shut up. I'm thinking,' Stolcher snapped.

They wanted orders, of course. He momentarily cursed the way the Nazis discouraged free-thinking and initiative; it was perhaps the most short-sighted aspect of fascism in his eyes. A thousand thoughts flooded his mind and he fought to make sense of them. What to do with the bodies? Then there was a search to organise and, god-forbid, his boss should find out before he'd dealt with it. There was absolutely no way this woman could be permitted to reach safety; that was his single priority now. He turned to the major and rattled off a series of orders.

'Detail someone to attend to the burials. But first contact the office of the Military Governor and tell them to place security checkpoints on every road out of the city. Do it now.'

'Jawohl, Herr Hauptsturmfuhrer.'

'If Stülpnagel raises any objections, tell him that this is a Gestapo-run operation. That ought to put a stopper in his complaints. Finally, call 711th Division Headquarters and get a company of troops for a cordon and search operation.'

'But that's a static division, they're for occupation duties only.'

'I don't want to launch an invasion of the British Isles, you moron. I just need soldiers in trucks. If I wanted your opinion, I'd give it to you. Map!' This last was yelled out loud and sent the idlers in the courtyard into a flurry of activity. A selection of maps arrived shortly thereafter and, spread across the bonnet of the truck, Stolcher searched through them. At 1:25,000 scale, it took a while before he located the map sheet he needed. He jabbed it triumphantly.

'Here is our target,' Stolcher addressed the harassed major, 'But you must tell 711th Division that they are not to enter the village under any circumstances, *verstehen*? I want them to cut off the roads leading in by 2000 hours tonight and await my arrival.'

'*Verstanden*. But I can't see the name of the village, your finger is in the way.'

'It's called Chambois-le-Fue.'

Chapter Thirteen

The sky was a deep crimson streak when Peter arrived at the Station's maintenance hangar on the north side of the airfield. The dayshift had concluded and airmen in dark overalls streamed out towards the domestic site. To their warm ale in the N.A.A.F.I. and perhaps some music or even dancing, he wondered jealously. To his satisfaction, he saw that his Lysander was parked out on the hardstanding next to the hangar, alongside a couple of Spitfires belonging to the Tangmere Wing.

'Right, I'll have to sweet-talk the Eng Controller. You climb in and stay out of sight.'

'I'll need a hand with these bags,' replied Sutherland, who had driven them.

It was the first time Peter had set eyes on the two large canvas bags in the back of the Austin.

'What's in them? Nothing contentious?'

'Oh no, nothing contentious. But what do you mean by contentious?'

'Just anything that's likely to damage the aircraft in flight.'

'Oh, it's all contentious then. Take a look.'

Peter pulled the cords open on the nearest bag and peered in to find the slim, metallic bodies of several sub-machine guns, boxes of ammunition and the grim shapes of what could only be hand grenades all crammed in together. The other contained a Bren light machine gun, magazines for same, and cardboard packs marked 'Composition B'.

'What's that?'

'It's explosive.'

'Do we really need all this? You've got enough explosive to

start a war here.'

'Peter, we're *in* a war. We've got no idea what's waiting for us in France, but you can't really expect the Krauts to just let us wonder in and collect Eve as easy as kiss your hand, can you?'

'Well no-'

'Good. Remember, forearmed is forewarned. So, we must hope for the best and prepare for the worst. What we don't use we can give to our Resistance helpers.'

'We've got helpers then?'

'Of course we have,' Sutherland said with an impatient tone creeping into his voice. 'Now are we going to sit here chatting all night or are we going to rescue Eve?'

The apron was deserted as Peter crept towards the Lysander, carrying one of the heavy bags over his shoulder. The Bren's barrel stuck painfully into his armpit as he carried it and he felt blissful relief when he set it down next to the aircraft. Peter climbed the first rung on the aircraft's boarding ladder, unlatched the rear canopy and slid it back to its furthest position. Sutherland climbed in, surprising Peter with how quickly he moved, and whispered for the bags. When they were in, Peter pulled the canopy shut and walked off to the hangar.

The Engineering Controller occupied a communal office on the airfield side of the hangar. Peter paused outside and listened to the jazz music playing on the other side of the door, along with the cheery banter of men at work. He set his cap on his head, buttoned his Mae West, and cleared his throat. For this to work, he reflected, he would need to play it very fast and loose.

'Good evening, chaps,' Peter said, slamming the door open intentionally. 'Oh, I'm not interrupting, am I?'

There were four men in the office. None had been expecting a visitor, or so Peter concluded from their relaxed attitudes and half-dress. One of the engineers slowly withdrew his heels from the desk in front of Peter and stood, self-consciously scratching his neck where his tie should have been.

'Good evening, sir. How can I help you?'

'I'm doing the air test on the Lizzie, can you chuck me the Form 700? I'll sign her out and be on my way.'

The engineer gave his mates a look and one of them turned the wireless down. He glanced in the log in front of him and made a face, 'The air test is scheduled for tomorrow morning, sir. No-one briefed it had been brought forward.'

'Oh, that's annoying. Is she ready to go?'

'Well, yes sir. She's been fuelled but normally the Engineering Officer looks over the paperwork before we hand over the aircraft.'

'This aircraft is due for operations tonight, pending the outcome of this air test.'

The man cleared his throat, 'As I said, we wasn't informed. I should really call the Engineering Officer.'

'If you must. But you'll need to get a shift on, I want to be away before the hour. It's operationally vital.' Peter nodded at the clock on the wall that read 2147 hours. He didn't feel too bad because technically nothing he'd said was an outright fib. But neither was it the truth. His mask threatened to slip when he caught sight of the distraught look etched on the engineer's face as he mulled over his options. He was undoubtedly weighing up whether it was more hassle to disturb the Engineering Officer, who was likely several gins into his evening in the Mess, or just sign out the aircraft.

'Do you want the telephone number for Mess reception?'

'Oh, no need for that, sir. She's booked for an air test; I'll fetch you the 700.'

'Thank you,' Peter replied with a smile. He was delighted that the ruse had come off, and more than a little relieved. He signed his own name in the Form 700 to take responsibility for the aircraft and turned to leave. As he pulled the door open, there was a shout behind him.

'Wait a minute, sir,' the engineer called.

Peter stopped, his heart frozen. He turned around casually and forced a smile.

'Yes?'

'Your helmet sir,' the engineer replied, handing him his leather flying helmet, 'You wouldn't want to take-off without that.'

Peter marched stiffly towards the Lysander, which stood out as a black shadow against the darkening sky, half-expecting to be called back at any second. There was a pencil line of purple on the horizon, the last vestige of the day, and over his shoulder the waxing moon had snuck up. There would be good moonlight to show him the way, he told himself.

Peter performed a quick walkround, then climbed up to the tall cockpit, slid the glass back, and clambered in. As he strapped in, he hissed to Sutherland, 'Keep your head down; we're not out of the woods quite yet.'

A couple of 'erks were led out of the hangar by a sergeant and Peter stuck his head out of the window to tell them he was ready to start. He pushed the fuel primer three times and waited as the ground crew turned the propellor. When they stood clear, the Sergeant gave Peter a thumbs-up and he added a final squirt of primer before switching the magnetos to 'on'. He hit the starter button and the engine coughed a couple of times. There was a pop and then an almighty bang, accompanied by a cloud of black smoke. Then the propellor was spinning and the big Mercury engine purred with its distinctive growl. Peter smiled to himself, it felt good to be back in the cockpit.

A quick glance at the instruments told him they were in working order and pressures and temperatures were all normal. Peter had no desire to stick around, not least because the Lysander's engine disliked being sat idle. He signalled for the 'erks to remove the chocks. When he saw they were clear and holding the wooden blocks, he gave them a wave, released the parking brake and gently nudged the throttle forward to begin a fast taxi.

As the Lizzie skittered along the perimeter track, Peter called the tower over the wireless to ask for permission to take-off. After a short pause, a bored-sounding voice replied with the details of the active runway and his departure approval. Tangmere had become thoroughly used to the odd ways of its Special Duties lodger, and this request warranted no special attention. The flarepath twinkled in the darkness, a reminder of the dangers faced by aviators at night, when senses were dimmed and peril lurked everywhere.

'You better strap in now,' Peter yelled over his shoulder as he braked the left wheel to swing onto the runway. He ran quickly through the checks, then he unfolded his map and placed it over his left knee.

'Strap in how? There's nothing back here to strap into,' Sutherland shouted over the fuel tank that divided the front cockpit from the rear.

'In that case, hold on tight.' Peter advanced the throttle to take-off R.P.M. and held the stick firmly in the centre. The engine burbled and the purr grew to a mighty roar. He released the brakes. The Lysander was built for this sort of thing and set off down the runway in a trice. It required very little rudder input and the ease with which the magnificent machine powered into the air filled Peter with pleasant anticipation. This was his domain, his time.

The flarepath became a blur. There was an audible clack as the flaps and slats retracted and the ground dropped away. The few visible landmarks diminished rapidly. He made a gentle turn south, climbing over a lane and fields, then the darkness below was replaced by a glassy mirror as moonlight reflected off the sea. He levelled out at 300 feet and looked out towards the enemy coast. It was not fog-bound this evening, a few clouds scudded across the sky, but they were thousands of feet higher up.

It was only now that he could consider the magnitude of what lay ahead. Misleading his superiors and pinching an aircraft were nothing compared to the prospect of landing in occupied France and taking on the German army at first-hand. Even with some handy Resistance muscle to help them, this was going to be one hell of an undertaking.

*

Eve winced as she washed her blood-stained clothes by the light of a single electric bulb in the little sink of the apartment, which constituted the only safe place she knew in Paris. But here in St. Germain, her safety was neither assured nor everlasting. The Gestapo had taken her possessions from her and must certainly have turned over her attic room near Montparnasse, along with the unfortunate Madame Foulon. Eve reminded herself that Foulon knew nothing, however, and her ignorance would be her salvation, so long as she kept private her hatred of the Germans.

Her body felt raw and tender thanks to the beating she'd taken in the back of the truck. She was also desperately hungry, having been deprived of food for more than 24 hours now. The lorry driver who helped her escape had generously given her some bread rubbed with garlic, which she devoured underneath her tarpaulin. But still her stomach growled and threatened to derail her thought process as she planned her next moves.

Plainfare had confirmed their suspicions. Grapple was a bust and S.O.E. was being played by a devious Gestapo agent called Stolcher. Eve recognised the man from her abortive interrogation at Avenue Foch. She had a clear picture of the weaselly, balding and chubby little Kraut in her mind. All of

Grapple's agents, including their French helpers were being held in Fresnes. 53 people in total. Should Eve make a successful getaway, their fates were sealed, one way or another. Plainfare had been unambiguous in his instructions, she was to tell her superiors to order the RAF to bomb Fresnes immediately, thereby denying the Gestapo any further intelligence value from their prisoners.

Before any of that could happen, she reminded herself, she had to get out. Her only hope was to use the escape route she'd been provided with by Sutherland. But that route belonged to Grapple and, therefore, it was as blown as everything else touched by the network. Including the safehouse she sheltered in.

A dog barking down the street caused her to freeze and listen for other sounds that foretold the approach of a seizure team. After a few minutes she was satisfied that it was nothing untoward. Still, there was no sense tarrying here. She had quite a way to go. She tried to remember the lines of a Robert Frost poem she had learned at school; it seemed apt. Although she wracked her brain, the title was just beyond her recollection.

She forced her mind back to the present. Her first priority was to alert Sutherland that she required extraction, then she had to make her way to the landing ground near Chambois-le-Fue. The first part was easy, there was a wireless set concealed beneath the floorboards in this very room. The second was going to be harder. For one thing, Stolcher almost certainly knew the details of the escape route and was several hours ahead of her. That meant he would be able to shut down all the major roads out of the city and probably had people at all the train stations.

After squeezing the water out of her clothes, she assembled the transmitter and sent a short message that simply gave the time of the rendezvous. There was no way she could make it tonight, even if it was possible to organise a pick-up. So the rendezvous was set for two nights' time, which would be a Friday, if her recollection was correct. She added that she would be 'accompanied', knowing that Sutherland would pick up on that nuance and respond accordingly. When it was done, she slammed the set repeatedly against the wall until it was no longer operable and stuffed it back into its hole.

Her clothes were still damp and clung uncomfortably to her as she dressed. She pulled the bedclothes from the bed and tore the sheets into strips to wrap around her feet, binding them with aerial wires torn from the wall. Then she wrapped the blanket around her shawl-fashion, like a beggar woman, and stepped out onto the darkened street.

Eve shuffled along urgently, but not so quickly that it might attract undue attention. If the roads and rail were closed to her, she had only one other option. On foot it was 40, 45 minutes at the most, to the Pont Neuf. On the way, a pack of wicked children ran after her and yelled abuse. They were chased off by a laughing party of off-duty German soldiers who bumped into her as she limped along with her hand out. For a moment her heart was in her mouth. To have come so far only to be caught by accident in the last furlough; she was too enraged to feel scared. But then they were past her, making dirty jokes and calling to one another in voices that faded as they stumbled on down the street.

She paused in an alleyway, gathering her shawl about her. The smell of urine and rotting food met her nostrils and she wrinkled her nose at it. Dark forms lurked at the end, revealed only by the glow of their cigarettes. Eve decided it was perilous to linger and, her stamina recovered, she set off again. The Pont Neuf appeared at the end of the road, tantalisingly close.

The urge to throw off her disguise and run for it was overwhelming. She forced herself to walk even as she heard the deep chugging noise she had prayed for echoing up from the

Seine. The bridge was dimly illuminated by a handful of lights along its length. They revealed the hunched forms of several couples locked in tight embraces in the refuges on both sides. The city of love, she smiled to herself. A *Kubelwagen* puttered by, a pair of fat German officers in the back too deep in conversation to notice the tramp who vaulted the parapet and threw herself into the river.

The sensation of falling lasted a fraction of a second. The drop was cut short by the barge passing beneath the central span and Eve landed comfortably on the canvas hold cover. She lay there for a moment, waiting for a shouted alarm or the fatal beam of an electric torch shined her way. But all she saw was the star-filled sky slipping along above her. She permitted herself a moment of congratulation as realised she really had slipped the net. Sleep threatened to overwhelm her, but she fought it back. And then, seemingly without reason, the words of the Robert Frost poem materialised in her mind.

But I have promises to keep,
And miles to go before I sleep,
And miles to go before I sleep.

Eve awoke the next morning to the seagulls squawking and sat bolt upright, worried she had slept so long that she had somehow reached the coast. She was relieved to find fields and woods on either side and, in the middle of wondering where she was, she was startled by a voice behind her.

'*Bonjour, madame, comment allez-vous ce matin*?'

'I'm so sorry, I didn't mean to stowaway on your boat. Your, ah, *bateau*? But I was in rather an urgent hurry, I'm afraid.'

The bargeman, who must have realised that ordinary tramps do not ordinarily fall from the sky, was the soul of discretion. He informed Eve they were just approaching Médan, but she might be better off disembarking north of the town quay if she wished to avoid the authorities. He was a kindly man who shared his simple breakfast of eggs and tomatoes with her and told her of his experience of working the river. He had a young crewman who minded the tiller, and between them they explained how little work there was now with the blockade and the Germans ruining the economy to feed their war. They had carried grain up from Le Havre, and meagre quantities of that, but eked out a living by moving contraband.

‘What sort of contraband do you transport?’

‘This and that,’ the bargeman replied with a shrug.

They brought the barge close-in some way above Médan, just long enough for Eve to leap onto dry land. She waved until it was returned and then set off across the fields in the direction she took to be roughly west.

It was with more than a little luck that she found herself walking the final few miles into Chambois-le-Fue. The first was the happenchance of being offered a lift by a doctor who was driving to Dreaux, almost half the distance she had to cover. That night she shared a farmer’s barn not far from Nueville with an indignant owl that hooted and shrieked at her but drew no undue attention. The next morning, she trekked across country as far as Breteuil, where a priest gave her a change of clothes, some coins from the poor box, and the Lord’s blessing. She waited in the church until the late afternoon before slipping out at dusk.

The road to Chambois-le-Fue was quiet, eerily so to Eve’s mind, and she left it with a couple of miles to go, preferring to approach through the countryside. Her plan was to rest up in the town until midnight, and then make her way onto the landing ground, some four miles further on down the road. She had memorised the map and could visualise the long, thin field with a stand of trees down one side. Her confidence of finding it in the dark was supreme, although she felt incredibly weary. She told herself it was lack of sleep or her poor diet, but a nagging doubt in the back of her mind reminded her that she was probably at least a month pregnant. Most women in this condition would be horrified at the risks she'd had to take with her health, but to Eve it was all necessary; she barely thought of herself once.

Few people could be seen in the market square, but voices brought together in song emanated from the church on the other side. She realised that it was Mass; that would account for why the little town appeared unexpectedly sleepy. On the northern side of the square, squeezed between the church and the town hall was a hotel, of sorts. A two-storey building with a wooden sign out front that claimed it was the Hotel du Lac. Eve could not remember seeing a lake anywhere nearby on the map, and assumed the name was arbitrary. She had sufficient money to pay for a room for one night, and at least it would get her off the street. After watching it for an hour or so, she decided to take the plunge.

There was no-one at the little reception desk in the foyer, no-one in the lounge, and no-one in the cramped restaurant. Eve's senses were awakening, when a youth appeared from a door behind the stairs and bid her *bon soir*. She asked for a room and paid the extortionate tariff up front. The boy asked her to sign the guest book without requesting her papers and Eve scribbled in an alias. Then he led her up the single stairwell to the first floor, where a half dozen bedrooms were located. Hers was at the end of the corridor and the boy pushed the door open and handed her the key.

'Don't you want to know if I'll be eating this evening?'

'*Pardon, Madame*,' he replied, blushing.

Eve thought she saw something in his eyes just in that instant that caused her alarm.

'Never mind. Just leave me undisturbed, please.' He nodded and was gone.

She closed the door behind her and leaned against it, knowing she should feel relief at this point but instead feeling a rising sense of anxiety that she'd made an error.

'Good evening again, miss.'

Eve swivelled to face the corner of the room where the voice had come from. Recognising, with mounting horror, the face of Erich Stolcher peering at her from a wicker chair. She placed a hand on the doorknob.

'I wouldn't do that if I were you,' Stolcher said, lifting his hand to reveal a Luger semi-automatic pistol. 'Away from the door.'

Eve raised her hands and backed slowly away from him.

'I suppose you want to handcuff me?'

'Yes, but don't think I'm stupid enough to come over there and do it myself. I saw what you did to my colleague.' Stolcher threw a pair of handcuffs that landed at Eve's feet, 'Put them on.'

As she picked up the heavy cuffs, Stolcher stood and pulled a black leather briefcase onto the bed. From this he produced a canvas roll, similar to the type used by carpenters. When he unrolled it, the contents glinted at her; it contained unspeakable instruments of torture. Stolcher's face lit up at her reaction and he said in a voice dripping with malevolence, 'And then we're going to have a little chat about who you are and what you're doing here.'

Chapter Fourteen

Conscious of the threat from prowling night fighters, Peter brought the Lysander in low. Very low. At one point he had to pull back hard on the control column and advance the throttle to avoid a stand of trees, which appeared out of the gloom. He felt something thump the undercarriage as he passed them. Sutherland would be having a fit in the back, he grinned to himself.

He'd crossed the coast at Deauville, and then followed the line of the River Troques as far as Lisieux. From there he travelled across country by map and stopwatch, some 35 miles to the Foret de Breteuil. Here, he planned to orbit the forest in search of the lights of the landing ground. But he noticed the flarepath of the big airfield at Evreux way off to the north-east first. Although the lights were not bright, he felt exposed and vulnerable by its mere proximity and found himself unconsciously drifting away to the south to put even more distance between them.

When he was sure he had found the right spot, he put the aircraft into a gentle left-hand turn and flashed the landing lights in imitation of the aircraft's Morse code letter. He scanned beneath them, but nothing shone back.

'Keep your eyes out for the signal,' he shouted back to Sutherland.

Peter was almost certain he could identify the landing field even without a signal. The moonlight was so strong that visibility was excellent. For that reason, his eyes kept returning to the same patch of ground.

'I thought I saw something there, just a moment ago,' Sutherland said.

'Where?'

'It was at nine o'clock but more like six now.'

Peter shook his head; this wasn't promising. It was hardly like they could just turn around and go back. Neither could they sit flying circles in the sky indefinitely. On the next pass, Peter saw it, a lone tiny light twinkling out the Morse code letter J in response, but no landing lights. He chopped the throttle, so the big engine's roar reduced to a purr again, passed the field overhead and entered a descending right turn to bring him back onto his final approach into wind.

'Sit tight, we'll be down in three minutes.'

Flying the Lizzie was like a cross between driving a London bus and riding a moving staircase, he mused to himself as the field reappeared just above the instrument panel. The wind turned out to be just north of east and he applied a little right rudder to stay lined up on the field, but otherwise the approach was textbook. He held the control column firm, trimmed back as he passed through 100 feet and the flaps and slats popped out. With a gentle bump they were down in enemy territory, rolling smoothly along the field as the airspeed bled off.

Peter did not need to apply brakes, the aircraft stopped well before the hedge at the end of the field. Off to the right of the nose, dark figures ran towards him. He dropped the cockpit glass on both sides and reached down to his boot, where he'd stuffed his revolver. Two of them stopped short to permit a solitary figure to jog forward under the wing and mount the strut, presumably to talk. Peter pointed the pistol out of the cockpit so that it was directed straight at the heart of his prospective liaison.

'Steady on,' the figure said.

'Christ almighty,' Peter replied, recognising Charlie hanging there in the cockpit window.

'Watch that thing doesn't go off,' Charlie grinned. 'It would be a very strange way to end a successful escape attempt. Don't you think?'

After taxiing back to the end of the field, Peter shut the aircraft down and climbed out to help unload the equipment. Charlie threw his arms around Peter who, caught off guard, responded weakly with, 'Delighted to see you looking so well, old chap.'

As Sutherland handed out the bags, Charlie introduced his friends.

'Peter, this is Victor Resonet. He's with the Resistance and works with one of the intelligence organisations. And this is Jean Morvan. His deputy.'

'Pleased to meet you both. Where's the rest of your force?'

'I have another two posted in observation of the town, and then there are the five of us,' Victor smiled.

'Seven? We're taking on the Germans with seven men? They must have at least a battalion to patrol this area,' Peter said, shaking his head.

'It's more like a platoon,' Victor replied. 'We think no more than 40, judging by the number of trucks they arrived in.'

'Oh well, that's much better,' Peter said sarcastically.

Jean was laying out the contents of the two bags on the ground next to the aircraft and he whispered, 'Oui, but we have a company's worth of firepower here. And enough explosive to level the entire town. We will be fine; *allez*!'

Peter looked doubtful, but Sutherland pushed past him to shake Victor's hand warmly, 'I'm so glad you could come, thank you.'

'No problem. Do you want to talk through the situation?'

'Certainly. Peter, Charlie, if you sort out the weapons, I'll bring you over for a briefing shortly.' Sutherland marched off to the nearby woods with Victor and Jean.

'I have to say it's damned good to see you,' Charlie said as he sorted through the sub-machine guns.

'Likewise, I thought you were dead. You know, I'd heard you had a spot of bother on your training unit and I pulled some strings to get you onto operations. I was feeling awful about it.'

'Well, actually it seemed to work out more or less for the better.'

'Really, how so?'

'Well the crate got shot down on our first outing. I don't think anyone got out, but I ended up hiding with a French family. On their farm. There was a girl there, called Cecile-'

'There usually is with you, Charlie.'

'No. I mean, not like that. Well, a bit like that. Look, you can hardly talk. Good old rule-following Peter Denhay. A man who never put a foot wrong before and here he is at the controls of a stolen aeroplane.'

'What?' Peter attempted a confident laugh of denial, but it came out as an awkward guffaw.

'Deny it if you want. But I can hardly believe Bomber Command just let you borrow a Lysander to go rescue your girlfriend from the Nazis. "By all means, old chap, don't bring it back too pranged", they never said. How the worm has turned for you.'

Peter said nothing in reply.

'I thought so. Anyway-,' Charlie grinned at his friend's discomfort as he loaded another magazine with 9mm rounds, 'I'm glad you're here. Otherwise I'd never have the opportunity to apologise for being awful to you when we returned to England. I've been below par, but I'm feeling better now.'

'I'm glad to hear it. Have you been fighting? You look like you've got a black eye?'

'Oh yes, that. I never mentioned that Cecile was pretty sweet on me too, but there was some awful creature on the farm who threatened to denounce us to the Krauts. So, we had to put him away.'

'"Put him away", how?'

'Cecile hit him with a spade and that seemed to do the trick in all honesty. After that I came here. Well, via Rennes where I met up with Victor's gang. Rum fellows these Resistance types, there's all sorts here. I helped them flash the signal to you. They're hopeless at Morse, you know.'

Sutherland hissed, 'Are you two finished yet?' He'd approached silently from the woods.

'Sure. There's eight Thompson sub-machine guns, six magazines a piece. Ten hand grenades. The Bren, of course, with ten magazines – they'll need to go easy on those. And then the Composition B, twelve bars of that.'

'Good enough for government work,' Sutherland said.

'What's the plan?'

'Come with me, you'll like this.'

Inside the woods, Sutherland led them to where Victor and Jean squatted at the edge of a clearing. The moon shone on a tiny model created from earth, twigs, and rocks.

'This is a map of Chambois-le-Fue,' Victor said in a low voice. 'You see the town is divided in two by this river here. The river isn't deep and can be forded above the town. A simple stone bridge links the northern end to the southern.' Victor pointed to the village, marked out in rocks. It was not unlike the figure eight, with the larger oval in the north.

'Here in the south, the Germans are using l'Auberge Du Nord, a guesthouse, as a field post. In the northern end, they have rounded up the townsfolk and are guarding them inside the church. We believe your agent is being held in this hotel on the main square.'

'Well, what are we waiting for?'

'Hold your horses, Peter,' Sutherland said. 'Fools rush in where angels fear to tread.'

'For this to succeed, it will require much cunning and a great deal of dash,' Victor smiled.

'You have a plan then?'

'My men and I will create a diversion, here in the south,' Victor pointed at l'Auberge Du Nord. 'That will draw the Germans from the north towards it, where we will spring a trap. Giving you the opportunity to slip into the hotel across the gardens to the rear and set your agent free. Then we make our way back to the landing ground via the river road we used to enter the town.'

'What about Jerry reinforcements? I presume they've stationed more troops within driving distance,' Charlie said.

Victor shook his head, 'The nearest Bosches are in Argentan and would take most of the night to get here. Even if they have time to raise the alarm. We'll need all the explosive and the machine gun, *d'accord*?'

'Yes, and what happens if it doesn't go to plan?' Sutherland said, stuffing a hand grenade into his jacket pocket.

'Jesus, you're actually enjoying this, aren't you?'

'What's not to enjoy, Peter? A walk in the moonlight, a little rugger-mugger with Jerry. You've got your whole life to sit at a desk, my boy.'

'Well, what's left of it,' Charlie grinned.

Victor looked displeased and interrupted, 'If we come up against unexpected resistance or something goes wrong, we fight our way out. If Peter is killed or injured, we destroy the plane and try to escape on foot. In any eventuality, my men and I will not be returning to England with you.'

'What?' Now it was Sutherland's turn to be surprised.

'I know you're fond of stoking resistance from home, but the embers will never take fire unless there are people here to lead it; I stay with them,' Victor nodded to Jean, who smiled proudly.

'Very well. In that case, gentlemen, I think we should join the ladies.'

The group split about two miles down the river road. Victor and Jean faded into the bushes at the roadside leaving Peter, Charlie, and Sutherland to continue on to the ford, about three quarters of a mile from the town. In his heavy sheepskin flying jacket and boots, Peter was soon sweltering, but he had no other way of carrying the spare magazines and grenades he had collected.

'Just imagine if Sergeant Roskilly could see us now,' Charlie whispered as they marched along in Sutherland's wake.

'He'd never believe it, poor sod.'

'I'll say. Hey, where do you think he is now?'

'I imagine he went into the bag in Crete with all the others. If he was lucky.'

Charlie fell silent, but the crack of a branch ahead made Peter freeze. Sutherland dropped to one knee and brought his Thompson up to the aim. There was a rustling of bushes nearby and a badger emerged from the woods near the river. It slinked across the road and disappeared into the hedgerow on the other side.

'Silly sod,' Charlie muttered under his breath.

'Shhh,' Sutherland replied.

The ford proved to be knee high and they crossed it without splashing. Emerging in open country, Peter glimpsed the unmistakable outline of the town. Its stone walls were a snowy white in the reflected moonlight. Sutherland seemed to glide forward, half bent at the waist, whilst Charlie bounded along behind at a run-walk.

They reached the edge of the town after another ten minutes of forced marching and hunkered down to wait for something to happen. Peter judged the distance from the hedgerow they inhabited to the start of the dwellings to be a shade under 250 yards. Taken at a run, it could be covered in a minute or so. It was probably just over five minutes to the hotel, unless they encountered opposition. And the plan hinged on not encountering opposition, he reminded himself. He checked his watch, it was 2353 hrs.

Peter quietly removed the magazine from his sub-machine gun and checked the top round was seated correctly. Then he shoved it back into the magazine housing until he heard the click of the retaining latch. He checked the safety catch was on and snatched the cocking handle back to chamber a round. Seeing this, Charlie did the same. Sutherland scanned the horizon. Time seemed to drag by. By some quirk of nature, the wind carried German voices from the town square.

The urge to smoke was becoming overwhelming, but Charlie's gentle snoring distracted him. He was about to nudge him awake when there was a flash of light, quickly followed by an ear-shattering explosion. The shockwave passed through him leaving his ears ringing. A flaming tyre landed about 25 yards away, and then Sutherland was on his feet sprinting towards the houses.

'Fuck me, I can't hear a thing,' Charlie yelled behind him as Peter clambered to his feet and set off after Sutherland. He'd only taken a few paces when the unmistakable sound of the Bren opened up on the far side of the bridge. It was a slow, rhythmic sound easily distinguishable from the high pitched and more rapid-firing Thompsons that also added their noise to the cacophony in the south. Occasionally a single shot ran out in reply, but the weight of fire was evidently against the defenders.

'Victor's giving the Krauts what for,' Charlie said, sprinting past Peter to the corner of an alleyway that led down to the square. Sutherland slipped across to the other side where he motioned for them to wait. Peter craned his head around the corner and caught sight of a couple of Germans with rifles sprinting past the alley towards the bridge. An impressive fire to the south lit the streets with an eerie orange glow, casting long and dangerous shadows that danced and flickered in the night. There were shouts at the end of the street and someone cried out in German.

'Come on,' Sutherland shouted.

Peter ran across the alleyway and followed Sutherland over a fence to a high wall where he paused, waiting for a leg up. He slung the Thompson over his back, reached up to grab the ledge and pulled himself up. On the top, he helped Charlie up and then the two of them hauled Sutherland over. Peter winced from a sharp pain in his knee upon landing, but he could see the outline of the hotel ahead and he forged ahead to clear the way.

A thin passage ran between the hotel and its neighbour. Peter turned into it and almost collided with a German soldier clutching a rifle. They both jumped, but the German pulled his weapon up first and pulled the trigger, which gave a dead-man's click. Quickly recovering his wits, Peter fired from the hip and the German crumpled. But another appeared at the end of the passage and sprayed away wildly with a machine-pistol, forcing Peter to duck back out of sight.

'He's got the passageway covered, we need to go around,' Peter cried.

'Hang about,' Charlie replied, pulling a hand grenade out of his pocket.

'Do you know what you're doing with that?'

But Sutherland's question went unheard as Charlie removed the pin, watched the safety lever fly off, and stared dumbly at the device.

'Chuck it, you berk,' Peter yelled, and Charlie threw it underhand into the passageway. They barely had time to throw themselves into shelter before there was a sharp crack and a cloud of dust and debris passed over them. Coughing, Peter leaned around the corner to empty his magazine but there was no sign of the German now. Charlie pushed past him to the edge of the square. Leaning out, a fusillade of rifle fire met him, and rounds ricocheted off the nearby wall, encouraging him to retire.

'No luck this way, they've got us pegged.'

'What?' Peter's ears were still ringing, but his stomach somersaulted as the Bren's fire slowed and then ceased as if cut off. In the silence that followed, he thought he could hear German voices calling to one another. They were getting organised. A wave of relief washed over him when the Bren started up again after a moment or two, but its firing was much slower now. Victor was undoubtedly trying to conserve ammunition.

'We'll need to work our way around their flank and get to the entrance that way,' Peter yelled.

Sutherland shook his head, 'No, there's no bloody time for that. I'll put down some fire, you make a dash for it.' Without waiting for a reply, Sutherland braced himself at the corner of the passage and fired steady bursts in the Germans' direction. Peter took off, turned the corner and reached the doorway unharmed. But the glass shattered as someone inside fired a machine pistol out of the entrance. He leaned back, waited for the firing to stop and then lobbed a grenade in through the opening. The blast blew out the remaining ground floor windows and then Charlie sprayed the rest of his clip in for good measure.

Peter pushed past him and entered the lobby. Two Germans and a young boy sprawled grotesquely on the ground amid the devastation. The smell of blood and gore reached his nose and he wanted to retch. No-one had survived and he felt a momentary wave of nausea and anguish pass over him, before blinking it away. Now, he told himself, was not the time for regrets. All that would come later.

*

The art of interrogation, Stolcher thought, is about keeping someone convinced that their life is really worth the information they possess. In practice, of course, it never is. Anyone who spied on the Reich did so under a theoretical sentence of death and almost all knew it. Evelyn Moore knew it and had opted to cooperate, which is how Stolcher came to know her name. But Stolcher was no fool; all agents underwent resistance to interrogation training that sought to strengthen their resolve under pressure. He would get what he needed eventually and then he'd have the girl shot. No-one would ever know how close she had come to exposing Operation BALDUR.

He was getting bored with her breadcrumbs now. Like a hungry shark circling the debris of a shipwreck, he held off on his attack until it would be devastating.

'Tell me again, who sent you?'

'I've already told you that. I work for Major Ivor Jones in S.O.E.'s F-Section. He sent me to France.'

'Yes, it's just I don't believe you. I have someone inside S.O.E. and they've never heard of you. There's not even a record of someone with your name, if that is your name, having been through S.O.E.'s training school. And it's hardly like there's many of you.'

She glared back at him with undisguised hatred in her eyes and repeated her claim. Stolcher reached forward and slapped her hard across the face, like he had done before, feeling the momentary thrill it brought him to control someone like this.

Glancing at the clock he saw with surprise that it was nearly midnight. He decided that he would start on the instruments now, because he wanted to be back in Paris for breakfast. First though, he would smoke and wash his hands. He hated to have unclean hands. As he lit his cigarette, he studied the girl with the eye of a practised misogynist. She looked like she would be a terrible fuck. A nice face but far too skinny for his liking.

'What I can't understand is why Ivor Jones would send you to check on his other agents when he has absolutely no idea that he's talking to me. Every supply drop he's arranged, every message sent, every espionage job completed. It was all me. Grapple is more my work than his, so why become suspicious now?'

'Perhaps you made a mistake? No plan is perfect, they all come unstuck somewhere,' she replied.

'I don't think so, I planned this down to the minute. I even used real intelligence to lure Jones in. Did you know that?' Stolcher sensed he was straying from the path, but he had so few people to brag to and Moore would be dead before dawn in any event. He gestured to his briefcase on the bed, 'I baited the trap with real honey and he just kept coming back for more. That's the problem with academics – they can tell you what the circumference, weight, and volume of a jam jar is, but not how to open it.' He laughed at his little joke, which he'd heard someone else say years ago.

Eve turned to look at him as he washed his hands in a basin of water, 'If Ivor Jones isn't your man on the inside, who is? It's got to be someone who works for him.'

'Ha. You think I'd divulge information like that to you?'

'Well you don't plan to let me go, do you?

Stolcher was stumped for a reply, but spluttered, 'You will get a trial like everyone else.' He was immediately unhappy with the barefaced lie and felt that he should be the one asking the questions.

'There won't be a trial,' Eve stated, in a matter-of-fact tone.

For the first time since he'd arrived, Stolcher felt the icy cold hand of doubt. He needed to re-establish his dominance, or the interrogation was as good as over. He withdrew a slim metal saw from the canvas roll.

'There is no way out for you, you better just tell me everything now before I start work. Otherwise I intend to remove your finger-'

The explosion cut him off even before he finished his sentence. He blinked twice and then looked out of the window. He sniffed the air and got a faint whiff of smoke; something was on fire. Then he heard a machine gun – some way off but steady, by its slow thumping sound. He threw the door open and descended the steps at a run to the lobby and through to the lounge, where a couple of soldiers stood looking out the windows. Their table had been shoved out in a hurry by the spilt liquid on the floor.

'What's going on?'

Neither of them knew, they stood dumbly to attention before him. Stolcher ducked out of the room back into the lobby and opened the glass-panelled front door. A truck stood in the square with a couple of soldiers in the back, more of them were emerging from the church where they were guarding the townsfolk.

'Go and find out what's going on and report back to me,' he yelled, his voice cracking. Storming back into the lobby he ordered the soldiers in the lounge to make sure no-one got inside the hotel before turning to the stairs. He had only just opened the door to the room when he felt a pressure wave, then a sharp crack blew him over in a cloud of glass and dust. He'd heard grenades go off before and knew that he had a matter of seconds to prepare, if he was facing a determined attacker. It seemed unreal to him now, on the very cusp of accomplishing his plans. Unreal and unfair, he fumed. He picked himself up and staggered into the room.

The girl gave him a triumphal look, which filled him with uncontrollable rage. He grabbed his pistol off the bed and waved it at her, 'I-I should shoot you now, you whore.' Then he noticed his briefcase again. The briefcase containing the Op

BALDUR intelligence bait sat unguarded on the bed and he felt the blood drain out of his face at his own stupidity. He realised that it was all over for him as the sound of feet pounding on the stairs below grew louder.

Chapter Fifteen

Glass crunched under Peter's boots as he ascended the stairs. He knew the advantage of surprise was lost to them now and leaned around the corner warily, probing with the Thompson's barrel in expectation of a burst of fire at any second. Charlie was behind him, but that was cold comfort because it was *he* who would catch the first rounds if this was an ambush.

He reached the first floor unscathed and twisted to either side to get a view down the corridor in both directions without exposing himself. Light cast on the debris-littered floor betrayed that the door at the end of the corridor was open.

'Hold it there, my friend.'

It was a German, speaking English but with a strong accent. It made the hairs on the back of Peter's neck stand up. He had only once before been close enough to hear his enemy's voice, and that was enough.

'We've got the building surrounded. You better come out slowly with your hands up,' Peter shouted back.

'Or so you would wish me to believe. I have your agent here, if you are not prepared to play silly games you may see that she is quite well.'

Peter looked at Charlie, who shrugged.

'I'm coming to the door now. But be warned I'm not on my own,' Peter called. He walked slowly and determinedly to the doorway, the floorboards creaked as he went. Charlie moved quietly behind him.

'Come, look,' said the German. 'It is safe as long as you make no sudden moves.'

Peter stood in the doorway with the Thompson pointed towards the floor. There was Eve alright, she looked bruised but ok with a handkerchief tied around her mouth. Her eyes widened as she recognised him. Behind her was a stout man in a crumpled suit. He didn't look like the image of a blond superhuman that Peter had come to associate with Nazis, but he held a pistol to Eve's temple with a firm, unequivocal hand.

'We can be friends. We both want what each other has. So, I propose a trade.'

'What do you want in return for our agent?'

'My freedom. All I ask is safe passage out of here and your promise that you will not attempt to pursue me.'

'Seems reasonable. But who are you that I would want to pursue you in the first place?'

'My name is Erich Stolcher, but I am of no interest to you. I work in Reich security, I am a policeman.'

'It's just, where I'm standing, you seem to be quite interesting. How about you lay down the gun and come along quietly?'

Stolcher looked angry and shook his head, 'You should have just taken the deal when I offered it.' Peter saw the arm come up, felt the slowness of his own response and knew Stolcher would be faster. Then a gun fired, and for the second time Peter's ears rang at the report, so close to his head. And Stolcher cried out in pain and gripped his bloody hand with his other.

'You shot my hand,' he cried.

'Grab him,' Charlie yelled. But Stolcher was faster and launched himself headfirst out of the window with a twinkle of glass as he dove through. There was a faint rustling of bushes outside.

'Christ, he's making a run for it,' Charlie said from the window.

'What? I'm deaf, Charlie,' Peter shouted as he untied Eve's gag.

'Peter, I can't believe you came for me, my darling. And

Charlie too. But where's Jumbo?'

'He's outside holding off the Krauts,' Charlie answered, interrupting their embrace.

'Hadn't we better get hold of Stolcher?'

'No, leave him; he's had it when he makes it back to Paris, the vile dog. In any event, I want you to take me home so that I can share some wonderful news with you.'

'What is it?'

'Not now,' Eve replied, grabbing a leather briefcase from the bed. 'Once we get home.'

Mystified, Peter grabbed her hand and followed Charlie down the stairs. Out in the town, the gunfire had slackened leaving only the faint crackling of a large fire. Charlie called out to Sutherland, but there was no response. Peter scanned about and his eyes eventually fell on a figure slumped against the truck wheel. They ran over to him and saw that Sutherland was bleeding from a bullet wound in his hip, his Thompson lay across his lap and all his magazines were spent.

'I gave them what for,' he groaned.

'You certainly did,' Eve replied kneeling down next to him. 'I'll need something to apply pressure to this injury.'

'Let's get him in the truck. We can sort him out on the way,' Peter replied.

'Wait,' said Charlie. 'We've got to open the church first, we can't just leave those people in there.'

Charlie and Peter ran to the church, peered in through the door and, seeing no Germans about, shouted at them all to get out and leave town. People exited the pews in a hurry and were soon pouring down the steps.

Back at the truck, they helped Jumbo and Eve on board and, with Charlie at the wheel, pulled out of the square. Leaving the church behind they drove over the river, passing several crumpled German bodies on the bridge, apparently victims of

Victor's Bren. Ahead of them, the source of the fire was revealed. What remained of l'Auberge du Nord burned fiercely, sending ash and embers soaring into the night. In front was a shallow crater where the other truck had stood; the Frenchmen had made good use of the explosive. Peter wondered idly how many Germans had been inside the inn when it went up. It seemed a brutal way to go.

There was no sign of Victor or his fighters, so Peter told Charlie to take the river road and head back the way they came. As they made the turn, four figures were picked out by the truck's headlights. Charlie hit the brakes and the truck skidded to a halt.

'Victor, you gave me a fright. I thought it was Jerry,'

'We almost rinsed you down, Peter. No need to worry about the Hun, he's heading off across the fields towards Paris as fast as his jackboots will carry him,' Victor spat. 'You got your agent back?'

'We did, but Sutherland copped one. We need to get him to a doctor.'

'It's not wise to stay here, can you fly him out?'

'It sounds like our only option,' Peter replied.

'Very well then, friend,' Victor slapped the bonnet, 'Until next time.'

Charlie floored the accelerator, but the truck was painfully slow. It was still some long minutes before they rolled up at the landing ground where the Lysander sat patiently.

'You get the crate fired up, I'll help Eve get Sutherland on board,' Charlie said.

Peter climbed the leg strut into the cockpit. He ran through the pre-take off checks, praying that the Mercury engine would turn over at the first attempt and the large Dunlop tyres had not sunk into the earth. Behind him, Charlie and Eve lifted the half-lucid Sutherland into the passenger compartment and squeezed in with him.

'Ready?'

'Wait. Jumbo's trying to say something,' Eve replied.

'What is it?'

'It sounds like 'Northolt'. What's that?'

'It's an RAF station on the outskirts of London. I can't think why he'd want us to go there, though. Plenty of other stations are closer and have medical facilities,' Charlie said.

'If Jumbo says Northolt, then that's where we're going,' Eve replied.

'Fine. Who am I to argue with a lady?' Peter pulled on his flying helmet, switched the magnetos on and hit the starter. There was a loud cough, a crack, and the propellor spun up. Peter thumped the instrument panel with undisguised joy and pushed the throttle forward to take-off speed. The Lysander rumbled along and was soon bouncing across the hard earth.

The ground fell away, and Peter pushed the column forward. He didn't want to climb too high, particularly so close to Evreux. Flying due north, he aimed to pass around Rouen and then cross the coast at Dieppe. But as he approached the coast, he noticed a dark shape in the sky off to the east appeared to be shadowing them from afar. Peter adjusted course slightly southwards. He was keen to ensure that their stalker could draw no obvious conclusion about their purpose by scrutinising their course.

'You're heading off track,' Charlie said, tapping him on the shoulder.

'I know. I think we've got company.'

'Can't you lose him?'

'Where? It's a gin-clear night. If he gets close enough, he'll smoke we're not a Jerry and then we're in trouble.'

'Isn't there *anything* you can do?'

Peter tried to recall something he'd heard Colin say, about

how one of the pick-up pilots had confused German air defences by showing a private signal. It was a slim chance, but there were no other options. He reached down to locate the Very pistol in the pocket beneath his seat, then he slid his cockpit glass down, pointed the flare gun out above the slipstream, and pulled the trigger.

There was a loud pop and then a bright red light soared above and behind them, as the flare descended slowly to earth on its little parachute. Peter glanced over to the dark shadow in the east, holding firm on its interception course. They would likely meet somewhere south of Dieppe at this rate. But then the shadow widened and the aircraft picture changed as it rolled away from them in search of another target. They'd spoofed him with his own signal.

The Lysander touched down on RAF Northolt's grass aerodrome after an hour's flying time. Peter never bothered contacting Fighter Command to inform them that he was on the way. He only called Northolt tower when he was inside the circuit and could see the flarepath shining back at him. The shocked duty staff recovered quickly after their unplanned arrival, sending out an ambulance and waking the Medical Officer.

Sutherland was shortly on his way, leaving Peter, Charlie and Eve with the Lysander to answer any difficult questions. A blue Austin pulled up flying the Station Commander's pennant on its bonnet and Peter inwardly said to himself, 'Here we go.' But the man who climbed out of the car surprised them all.

'Hullo, Peter. Jumbo told me that I might get a visit from you.'

'My word, its Wing Commander Cranmer. I mean, Group Captain Cranmer, sir. I had no idea you were here.' Cranmer, or Lord Aberdair as he was actually known, had helped Peter and Charlie to escape from behind German lines in Greece in his private aeroplane. None of them knew he had returned to Great

Britain.

'That was all part of the plan. Jumbo was worried he might not make it back and he didn't want you to take all the heat if it went wrong. He explained the mission to me, and I've got a few strings to pull on your behalf.'

'So, no disciplinary action, sir?'

'No. Although your time with 1419 Flight is probably over. You've given your boss an uncomfortable night, after all. But I dare say it was worth it,' Cranmer glanced at Eve and smiled.

'There's something else,' Eve replied. 'We have to tell S.O.E. about how Grapple has been penetrated. But before that, we have to bomb Fresnes Prison.'

Cranmer pushed his braid-covered cap back on his head and studied Eve, 'Let's get you all a cup of chocolate and then we can discuss this. Jumbo made no mention of a follow-on operation.'

Crammed into the Commanding Officer's car, they headed off to the Mess, where the staff were preparing hot drinks and rooms for the new arrivals. In the back of the car, Eve rested her head against Peter's shoulder.

'What were you going to tell me?'

'Oh, the good news? Peter, I'm carrying our baby.'

The car's brakes squealed for a moment before Cranmer looked back to the road.

'I-I don't know what to say, that's fabulous news,' Peter replied, realising it was his truthful opinion only as he said it.

'Congratulations to both of you,' Charlie grinned from the front seat. 'I always enjoy a September wedding.'

Peter cleared his throat, but the car pulled up at the Mess before he could say any more.

Chapter Sixteen

London, September 1941

The long, low-ceilinged room hummed with the noise of air being forced down subterranean vents. Its roof was reinforced with steel to protect it from air attack. It was in this secretive and armoured bastion that orders were devised that sent squadrons of bombers to their targets across occupied Europe. Here too, the staff of Bomber Command briefed the Air Officer Commanding-in-Chief, Air Marshal Sir Richard Peirse, on the progress of those operations against the Reich. Today, the assortment of staff officers who normally occupied the chairs along the sides of the room had been banished because a special operation was in contemplation.

On the long table in the centre sat a large-scale map depicting south east England and much of northern France. On top of that was a smaller map of Paris and, in Sir Richard's hands, an aerial photograph of Fresnes Prison. Tall and thin, Charlie thought Sir Richard had an unusual look of intelligence about him as he scrutinised it with his blue eyes. In the background a portly air commodore named Heppenstall droned on about bomb loads and weight of effort in a whiney, officious tone. A couple of group captains had been brought in too, Charlie suspected to 'stuff' the meeting. Otherwise the Bomber Command officers would have been outnumbered, although crucially not outranked, by the four people sat across the room from them.

Their seating arrangement did little to ease the adversarial tone of the meeting. At first Bomber Command wanted no part in the mission at all and referred to it as a 'diversion'. But Cranmer had name-dropped several senior figures in the intelligence community, and Sir Richard sat up. Now they were at least talking practically about how they might accomplish the objective, although Air Commodore Heppenstall's views on the merits of a two-squadron operation were at odds with his own views.

In one of those bizarre coincidences, Charlie recognised Heppenstall from before the war. He distinctly remembered being asked to leave his house in Chelsea in 1938, having made a bold but ultimately unsuccessful pass at his daughter at a drinks reception. In between pauses, Heppenstall glared at Charlie, who hoped the moustache he had grown in the intervening three years was adequate camouflage.

Charlie waited until Heppenstall was in the midst of a long, torturous monologue on bombing and interrupted, 'Excuse me, sir,' he addressed Sir Richard. 'But I've recently flown with the Main Force and our actual bombing accuracy by night is pretty appalling.'

Heppenstall blinked and stared at Charlie. The Commander-in-chief cleared his throat and asked, 'Who is this, Cranmer?'

'My name's Kendrick, sir. I've just come back from France after being shot down near Brest. I evaded the enemy for over a month,' Charlie replied, ignoring the fact that the question was not directed at him.

'I see,' replied Sir Richard. 'Go on then.'

'Well, I flew a night operation and it appeared to me that hardly any of the attacking aircraft managed to land a direct hit. If you really want a successful strike, you'll need to use many aircraft or make repeated attempts to attack the place. Even then you might not get anywhere.'

Heppenstall, whose entire head had turned an ugly beetroot colour, snapped, 'Well, we'll attack in daylight then. The aircraft are designed for it.'

'I don't think that's advisable,' Peter chimed in. 'Northern

France is just littered with German fighter bases. The casualties in any force attacking by daylight would be enormous. It means you would have to throw even more aircraft at it and accept high losses.'

One of the group captains whispered in Sir Richard's ear. Charlie could not hear the specifics of what was discussed, but it was clear that some new report had been published that was pertinent to the present discussion. Sir Richard nodded sagely, then said, 'It appears you might be onto something here. But I'm stumped if I can think of an answer for you.'

'Please sir, may I suggest something?'

Charlie glanced at Peter with a broad grin, he sounded just like a schoolboy. Sir Richard nodded.

'Well, I can suggest one aircraft that might be perfect for the job. You've got the Mosquito, which can carry a decent bombload and, if my experience is correct, it'll outrun any Kraut fighters even on the straight and level.'

Charlie frowned, 'A Mosquito?'

'I've seen it Charlie, it's wicked fast – trust me.'

Sir Richard interrupted, 'You have a plan?'

'Yes sir. A low-level daylight raid by three Mosquitos armed with 1,000 lbs bombs. We'll smash the prison walls to enable the Resistance to break in and free all the surviving Grapple agents.'

'Peter, that's an excellent idea,' Eve said. 'We can arrange for the Resistance to put in a local attack. With air support, it might just catch Jerry off guard.'

Heppenstall glowered, but Sir Richard clasped his hands and looked thoughtful. Eventually, he spoke, 'Bomber Command is just converting onto the bomber variant of the Mosquito now; I don't think we've officially declared any squadrons operational yet,' Sir Richard replied, glancing at Heppenstall who looked lost. The other group captain leaned forward to break the awkward silence, 'We expect 105 Squadron to be fully converted onto the B Mk. IV by November, sir. They have a handful of crews listed as limited combat ready now. Things fell behind when they lost their C.O. on that Stavanger raid-'

'Sir, I really must object,' Heppenstall interrupted, 'How can we expect 105 Squadron to get operational if we keep taking their crews away to fly raids?'

'It sounds like the perfect way to get a squadron operational,' Sir Richard said, with a wry smile. 'It's a lot to expect from newly converted crews, though. Can we make their lives easier at all?'

'*We* could lead it, sir,' Charlie said, without thinking. Inwardly, he cursed and tried to ignore Peter's ridiculous look of admiration. 'That is, Peter and I flew Blenheims together in Middle East Command. I'll warrant I could find the target at low-level and put our stick right on the guardroom.'

'They've got pedigree, sir,' Cranmer added, proceeding to explain to the Air Marshal how Peter and Charlie had raided the Luftwaffe advanced base at *Larissa* during the Greek campaign. Sir Richard raised an eyebrow, which Charlie took as something of a compliment from a man who wore the medal ribbons of the Distinguished Service Order and Air Force Cross on his tunic.

'Alright. You better signal RAF Swanton Morley with orders to prepare 105 Squadron for a special operation. No target details,' Sir Richard ordered. He stood to signal that the meeting was over and everyone else followed. As the others filed out, Sir Richard stepped forward to shake Peter and Charlie by the hand.

'Good luck, gentlemen. I dare say you'll need it.'

*

Tucked away in Norfolk's hinterland, RAF Swanton Morley was but one of the countless bomber stations strewn across the county. Its heart-shaped grass airfield bore three strips and it was home to an eclectic group of squadrons. 88 Squadron was equipped with the Douglas Boston light bomber, 152 Squadron operated the Spitfire Mk IIA, and 105 Squadron was in the process of converting onto the Mosquito. As with any unit converting to a new aircraft type, their aircraft were most visible in the circuit as Peter's car pulled onto the Station.

Charlie slept with his head against the glass, a deep rasping snore escaped from his nose. But Peter ignored him and wound down the window to look skyward as a pair of Mosquitos zoomed overhead. The throaty roar of their engines left a wide smile on his face. He barely waited for the car to pull up before he was out marching towards 105 Squadron's hangar. In the entranceway he met a civilian engineer in overalls and asked him for directions to the C.O.'s office.

'It's on the other side of the hangar, chum. But you won't find him there,' he chuckled. 'Takes an interest in the 'planes does our Wing Commander Merrick. Spends more time poking around in 'em than he does flying.' The man shook his head and walked off.

Peter found Merrick beneath a Mosquito with its port engine nacelle off, helping with an oil change. He was a gangly, ginger-haired fellow with a jolly face. Seeing Peter approach, he wiped his hands with a rag, tossed it at one of the engineers, and gripped his hand warmly.

'Teddy Merrick. You must be Denhay, delighted to meet you. I hear you've got a job for us?'

'Yes sir, but you won't thank me. It's a stinker.'

Merrick laughed and replied, 'Let me be the judge of that.' Catching Peter's look towards the Mosquito he smiled and said, 'You'll need to get familiarised with the aircraft. Have you flown anything like it before?'

'I've flown Blenheims.'

'Well at least you've handled a second engine. But the Mossie is something else again. Do you know her top speed is 380 mph? The Krauts have no idea what to do with the reconnaissance crates we send over.'

'What makes it so fast?'

Merrick gave him a mischievous look, 'Let me show you.'

Merrick led Peter over to the aircraft nearest the open hangar door, where a panel just aft of the nose bubble was open, and told him to climb in. Peter ascended the little ladder and sat in the green-painted nose section. Merrick's head appeared in the hatchway and he tapped the fuselage saying, 'Listen to this.'

'Good Lord, it sounds wooden.'

'It *is* wooden. It's a mixture of timber, plywood, and balsa. Makes her extraordinarily light so that, with these Rolls Royce Merlin XXIs strapped on, she's capable of doing 265 mph in the cruise.'

Peter whistled. The Blenheim could only do speeds like that in a flat-out dive.

'Do you know, the Air Ministry wanted to put a gun turret on it? Typical government over-specification,' Merrick said shaking his head. 'The boys at de Havilland came up with an outstanding aircraft and the RAF just *had* to interfere-.' Merrick stopped, perhaps feeling he was in danger of becoming a bore.

Peter looked about at his new office in wonder, then remembered the point of the conversation.

'Shall I take you through the mission, sir?'

'Yes, why not. Do you fancy a tea?'

They found Charlie outside Merrick's office. He'd cadged a brew from someone and looked quite refreshed after their overnight journey up from High Wycombe. A few others appeared at Merrick's behest, the crews of the other two aircraft joining in the raid. Aside from Merrick, the others had been hand-picked based on their flying proficiency and aircraft hours. Peter made the introductions and then outlined the mission to everyone.

When Peter came to the end of the briefing, he asked for questions. A tall, shaggy-haired Pole pointed to the aerial photographs of the prison and grunted, 'If all we have to do is knock down a wall, 1,000 lbs bombs are too big. If one goes even slightly off course, you could end up flattening a cell block.'

'We expect some collateral damage,' Charlie interjected.

'That's a good point, though,' Peter said. 'What would you advise?'

'Probably 500 lbs semi-armour piercing bombs with a delay fuse. I think 11 seconds should do it, enough for them to burrow their way into the wall. It should amplify the explosive effect.'

'Good thinking, Dubicki,' Merrick said.

'Do we have a fighter escort?'

Peter turned to the navigator who had asked the question.

'No. The plan is not to loiter long enough to need one. I'll lead the formation in, with the boss' permission, and put us over the prison. I'll pull up sharply to mark it, but you'll recognise it from this distinctive arrow-shaped outer wall and the cell blocks – they're four stories high. You both hit the outer wall while we orbit above at 500 feet and then make a run for it. If the wall isn't down after your attacks, we'll drop our bombs and scarper.'

'You want us to strike the western side?'

'Yes, you'll need to make your attack run from north to south, more to avoid hitting each other than anything else. We also need to time the attacks perfectly; with an 11 second delay on the bombs then 30 seconds between aircraft should be sufficient. You'll be at about 100 feet on your run in, so you want to avoid being blown up by someone else's bombs.'

'What about opposition?'

Charlie leaned forward, 'Jerry has a strong fighter presence in northern France. Me109s are most probable, but you might even find some Focke-Wulf 190s hanging around. They're quick, probably superior in performance to current marks of the Spitfire, but the plan is not to get into a scrap. Flak of course; we've modified the route to avoid large concentrations.'

Merrick continued, 'So, formation order is Denhay & Kendrick in the lead, Burrington and I as number two, and Walsh & Dubicki in the number three. When do you want to launch?'

'We've got to be over the target at first light and it's a flight time of one hour and 30 minutes; start engines at 0400 hours.'

'Very well,' Merrick replied. 'You need to get some hours on type if you don't want to end up a flaming pyre.'

The next day, Peter awoke in darkness to a gentle tapping on his door. He switched on the bedside lamp and squinted at his watch. 0300 hours. His head thumped from the five and a half hours he'd spent in the cockpit of aircraft serial GB-F, or F-Freddie, not to mention several glasses of Scotch he'd shared with Charlie, Merrick, and Dubicki in the Mess bar.

'Come in.'

Charlie's head appeared around the door, 'It's time.'

'Jesus, you look as fresh as a daisy.'

'Long practice, I dare say. Drinking, that is, not the early mornings.'

'Charlie?'

'Mmm?'

'We're doing the right thing, aren't we?'

Charlie glanced out into the empty corridor, then closed the door and slumped down on the empty bed opposite.

'You know, if we fly this mission there's a chance that some of our people will die. But if we don't, they'll all die. And not just put up against a wall in a "any last requests, old chap" sort of way. The Gestapo will put them through the worst imaginable torture to wring any final information out of them and *then* they'll smudge them out. It's more than likely that will lead to more arrests and further bloodshed.'

'I'm sick of this damned game of hide and seek. After this, I want to go back to normal flying,' Peter replied.

'Normal? Normal flying *is* hide and seek, Peter. It don't matter whether you're in Coastal, Bomber or Fighter Command, everyone's trying to catch the other guy out before he finds you and sends you spiralling down in flames. As far as I'm concerned, air combat is the most honest kind. It's not the game you should hate, brother, it's the damned war. Now put this on,' Charlie said, chucking Peter's battle dress jacket at him. 'And let's go start a prison break.'

*

'This *is* somewhat surprising, isn't it?'

Stolcher stood uneasily before Ritteln's desk. Subjectively, he could not agree more with his boss. It had been an uncomfortable night and day for him, spent hiding in bushes in the French countryside in fear of being captured and lynched by the Resistance. No less uncomfortable than the sensation of having the remains of his shattered middle and ring fingers snipped off by a doctor. Of all the suffering and indignity that had been visited upon him, it was this interview he welcomed the least. Ritteln had the power to make or break him, and he was about to learn which it would be.

'Herr Standartenfuhrer. I am aggrieved to have to advise you of the unexpected termination of Operation BALDUR and its likely exposure as a lure to the British.'

Ritteln cleared his throat, his face clouded with disappointment, 'It's worse than that. I have a report that 23 German soldiers were killed and 8 more injured at Chambois-le-Fue. Some of them, it adds, were disarmed and shot by members of the Resistance. What do you say to that?'

'They were supposed to act as my security detail. They didn't do their job and paid for their negligence with their lives.'

Ritteln harrumphed and set the report to one side. Stolcher took a deep breath and continued, 'I also lost the *ZINNMAN* portfolio in my attempt to escape.'

Ritteln did not explode, as Stolcher expected, but instead pushed himself away from the desk and stood up. He helped himself to a generous measure of brandy from a decanter and studied Stolcher, as if composing the words in his head that would follow.

'When I was in the orient, I learned that the Chinese have a proverb that is very apt. They say, "The flame that burns twice as bright, burns half as long". Have you heard that before?'

'No, Herr Standartenfuhrer,' Stolcher lied.

'Well I think we can both stop worrying about your flame burning too brightly now. You might think that I would have you sent off back east to help with the clearances of the ghettos but, you know, I think I'll keep you around.'

'I don't plan to be your errand boy,' Stolcher growled.

'Don't you? Perhaps you'd prefer to work with the *Einsatzgruppen* instead? Although, if it becomes known that you allowed top secret information to fall into the hands of the British, that would be one of the better outcomes for you.'

Stolcher said nothing. Seeing this, Ritteln sniffed and continued, 'So, I'll tell you how we're going to clean up your mess. First, we're going to send your agents off to a concentration camp to be dealt with.'

'But we've barely finished the interrogations – they still have intelligence value.'

'Their intelligence value is inconsequential compared to the message this sends to the Resistance about what happens when you interfere with matters of Reich security.'

'Herr Standartenfuhrer-'

'Shut up, Stolcher. I'm giving the orders here. I've already requested trucks and escorts from the Paris Garrison. Strangely, the 711th Division was unwilling to assist with further Gestapo operations. You'll accompany them tomorrow morning to Fresnes, load them up, and take them to the Gare de Lyon. A train awaits them there.'

Stolcher considered his options and realised that Ritteln held all the cards now. He had been defeated and must now submit to whatever terms he was offered. Frankly, he was somewhat amazed that he was not being marched out to the yard this minute with a firing squad following a sham trial. He had seen it enough times himself. Hell, he'd partaken in it.

'Jawohl.'

'Then you'll write up your report on Operation BALDUR, making it clear that one of your men compromised the operation. Guhr will do, he was killed recently?'

Stolcher made no reply but nodded his head.

'*Sehr gut,*' Ritteln continued, pouring another brandy. 'You know the terrible thing about ambition, Stolcher? It brings out the worst in people.'

Chapter Seventeen

'Angels 19. Make your heading 175 degrees. 20 minutes until next course change.'

Charlie glanced at Peter as he reduced the throttle and trimmed to enter the shallow dive that would see them flatten out at 100 feet just before the French coast. Looking back, he glimpsed the dark shapes of the other two aircraft in the formation trailing close behind. Strict radio silence was maintained to preserve the element of surprise. But the Germans were attuned to RAF intruder operations, since Fighter Command had been flying patrols over France from the previous year.

Charlie had no experience of flying these patrols, or the escorted bomber missions known as 'Circuses', but what he'd heard from the aircrew who had was not positive. Most common were grumbles about how little effect they appeared to have on the Luftwaffe, who still rose to meet them every time a crowd was sent over. In many respects, he thought, it sounded like a re-run of the Battle of Britain, only this time the tables were turned; the British were the attackers.

The patchwork of purple clouds around them thinned gradually as they approached Dover. He'd hoped it would have concealed their approach across the Channel, but the sky was practically clear once they'd left England behind and already the dawn was visible over Europe. He'd never been more ungrateful for an Indian summer. Glancing to his right, the coastline disappeared towards the Contentin Peninsular. He thought about the land that laid beyond that and pictured the lush rolling fields and salt-kissed beaches of Brittany, and Cecile.

'Enemy coast ahead,' Peter said, pulling him back to the present.

The grey-brown waters looked awfully close from the cockpit. There was something of a sea running, despite the otherwise calm weather. Over to the east, a freighter was making the most of the last hours of darkness to creep along inshore towards the Pas de Calais. Whether it would make it in time was doubtful, Coastal Command's Beaufighters would soon be prowling from their bases in East Anglia in search of a ripe target. A flash of colour below their feet and then they were skimming over green fields and hedgerows. The aspect of the coast changed as Peter rolled the aircraft to avoid Amiens and, without looking at the map, he knew they were passing Etaples. They swung south at Abbeville, where some furious light flak gunners blazed away at them in earnest, but vainly all the same. All three aircraft emerged unscathed and settled on a direct line towards Paris.

Peter was right, the aircraft was lightning quick; God knows how he was going to put their stick accurately on target travelling at this speed. He glanced up out of the canopy to check for fighters and saw nothing in the dawn's weak light.

'You know the other good thing about attacking at dawn, don't you?'

'What? No,' replied Peter without looking away from the horizon, painfully close at this level.

'Shift changeover.'

'What that's you say?'

'Jerry's just like us, regular as clockwork. As soon as the sun's up, the night fighters all get stood-down, the controllers go out for a smoke, and the engineers are off having a kip. Everyone's thinking about knocking off, and the day shift are barely awake. The perfect time to catch anyone on the hop, is shift changeover.'

Peter said nothing immediately, but then replied, 'Let's hope you're right.'

The terrain below them grew gradually more broken. Large forested areas appeared and, dotted here and there, were little towns and villages. They roared over them without a second glance, *Grandvilliers*, *Beauvais*, *La Chapelle*.

'How long to target?'

Charlie glanced at the map, 'Ten minutes.'

The Seine emerged from the dark far off to their right, snaking in tight silver coils as it reached the outskirts of the city. They climbed to crest a low ridge. Charlie felt a slight but insistent pressure push him into his seat and then they were over it. The sight on the other side drew an inadvertent gasp from his lips, for there was the great city laid out in panorama. Orange light reflected off the many buildings, which were picked out in pale white against the darkened streets below. Charlie had visited in his youth and picked out the Eiffel Tower first, then the Sacre Coeur beyond it.

'Target ahead,' he told Peter.

Fresnes stood out from the buildings that surrounded it, or rather the high cell blocks attracted Charlie's eyes first, then the arrow-shaped wall, and finally the long boulevard that ran parallel to the western wall, which they would strike. As they passed overhead, Charlie caught a glimpse of trucks and people in the yard staring up at them, but in a flash they were gone.

Peter keyed the radio, saying, 'Tally ho, tally ho.'

Although he'd been expecting it, Charlie was still surprised at the speed at which the Mosquito climbed. Blackness appeared at the edge of his vision and he fought to stay conscious, bending his head down to restore the blood flow. When the aircraft levelled out, he found he was able to glimpse the prison by craning over Peter's head as they circled.

'Here comes Merrick,' Peter said.

‘I can barely track him. He’s going too fast.’

‘Bomb release…it’s long. Jesus, he’s missed.’

‘Wait, wait. The bombs are on time delay, remember?’

‘There they go. Long, as I said; his approach was too fast.’

‘One of us should keep eyes peeled for Kraut fighters, don’t you think?’

Peter shot him a cold look, but he nodded in agreement. Common sense dictated it had to be Peter who would be look-out, he was flying the crate after all. If they got bounced, he would have to react immediately.

‘Dubicki rolling in now, a little high,’ Charlie said, leaning over for a better look. ‘He’s dropped. Bugger. Where did they go? Looked like at least one was near a cell block.’

An excruciating pause and then three explosions, two on either side of the wall and one direct hit on the nearest block. The dust and smoke concealed the scene below for a moment, when it settled it revealed the face of the cell block had fallen in a pile of debris.

‘The wall’s still up. They haven’t breached.

‘Looks like it’s down to us then. I’ll bring us in just above stall speed, use 120 mph for the release speed.’

‘Roger,’ Charlie replied, removing his straps and moving forward to the bomb aimer’s position in the nose. The aircraft rolled sharply to port and plunged towards the ground. As Charlie clambered forward, he felt an overwhelming sensation of unease as the fuselage narrowed around him to the Perspex nose canopy. In a flash, he clearly saw the nose section of his Whitley above Brest, spiralling as it was torn from the rest of the doomed aircraft. And he remembered the horrified face of the air gunner as his grip on the stringer weakened and he was flung away to be swallowed up by the night. Charlie slumped on the fuselage floor until the image passed, leaving him weak and shaking, his sweat-soaked uniform stuck to his body.

Charlie fought his own body to rise to his knees and crawl to the bombsight. He looked over it just as the aircraft levelled off from its performance dive. The streets surrounding the prison appeared to rise up almost to embrace the aircraft. Roofs flashed by, seemingly at touching distance. He adjusted the bombsight settings and plugged in his intercom lead just as Peter said, 'Standby, braking now.'

The engines throttled back and then there was a rumble as the undercarriage extended into the airflow. Charlie smiled to himself. It was a clever move to use the wheels as a pair of vast airbrakes. The aircraft shuddered, but continued on its flight towards the prison, albeit at a much-reduced speed. Charlie squinted down the sighting device as the prison wall slid into view; he grasped the bomb-release mechanism in his slippery hand and waited until the picture looked good.

*

The sun now popping up above the horizon presaged another one of those hot, uncomfortable days so common in Paris at this time of year. Stolcher much preferred spring, when there was at least a little moisture in the air still. He gazed out of the window of the black Mercedes 260 at the streets as they motored towards Fresnes and decided they looked more disgusting than usual. He'd long decided that Paris was a dirty city. Of course, the war didn't help with shortages of labour and materials, but he was forming the impression that nothing happened in the Occupied Zone without a German ordering it. What this city needs, he told himself and not for the first time, is a good downpour to wash away all the filth.

He had only just made this conclusion when he was brought sharply back into the present by his driver braking sharply.

'*Verzeihung*, Herr Hauptsturmfuhrer. The lorry in front-' the young man explained with a gesture at the rear of requisitioned Renault truck.'

He was in a black mood, a combination of being saddled with this chop job and the pain radiating from the cauterised stumps of his fingers. Concealing it from his driver made him feel weak and foolish, which only worsened his temper. Stolcher craned his head out the window to look around it but could only see the truck in front of that. He cursed, kicked his door open, and slid out of the vehicle. Storming down the column of vehicles, he rehearsed in his head what he would say to whichever *dummkopf* was holding up his task. Upon reaching the lead vehicle, he saw the prison gate remained closed and a knot of German soldiers stood in conversation with a jailer behind an open flap in the door.

'What's going on here? I demand to know the cause of this delay.'

An elderly, balding lieutenant turned around with a face like thunder to address him, then realised who he was talking to and clicked his heels to attention.

'The warders say that we do not have permission to remove prisoners without the consent of the authorities. They refuse to open the gate until we produce our credentials, Hauptsturmfuhrer.'

'What? I *am* the authority.' Red-faced, Stolcher reached into his jacket and pulled out his Luger, a gesture that caused the little crowd of *landsers* to part rapidly, to reveal the fat, moustachioed face of the recalcitrant guard.

'Now listen here, you oaf. I'm coming in to remove the prisoners marked on this list here, either with your consent or without it. If you and your family want to avoid the same fate as these people, I'd open the gate. Do it now.'

After a short pause, a metallic ringing announced that the gates were being unlatched and finally they swung open to admit the convoy. Stolcher smiled to himself, at least some people still recognised who's in charge around here. He stood in the shade of the gatehouse as the six trucks passed through the archway and parked, with typical German order, in a neat row awaiting their loads. The Mercedes was last through the gate and then the doors slammed shut behind them.

The Luger returned to its holster, Stolcher smoothed the prisoner list that he had crumpled in anger and tried to regain some of his composure. That was when he heard the air raid warning siren's eerie howl faintly, and from afar. He frowned, they were never attacked by day; this must be some kind of drill or rehearsal. So typical of the *Wehrmacht* to not bother informing anyone, he thought, and then he heard the low droning of an approaching aircraft. He barely had time to utter the words, '*Mein gott.*' The enemy had stolen a march on him.

The drivers and guards from the convoy were shouting and pointing skyward. Some sprinted for cover. With a roar, a twin-engine aircraft passed overhead. He caught a glimpse of a grey underbelly with British markings and an open bomb bay before his senses returned and he threw himself to the floor to await the resultant explosions. He heard the pitch of the aircraft's engines change as it turned and climbed away, but in its wake came silence. Nothing. A dud?

He stood and dusted his suit down, beginning to feel pretty smug that the enemy's one and only intervention was an impotent one. The series of explosions that followed knocked him off his feet. A house across the street from the prison gate disappeared and, in its place, a wicked conflagration raged in the featureless ruins. Smoke rose above the prison walls showing that the other bombs the aircraft carried had also detonated elsewhere.

He shouted at his escort, telling them to hurry to get the prisoners onto the trucks. He had no desire to be here any longer than he needed to be. But the words were barely out of his gullet before a second aircraft appeared. He threw himself to the floor once more as this one flitted over, but this time he actually saw the ordnance travelling through the air. One bomb clipped the bonnet of a truck, spinning it 90 degrees as if flicked by a giant hand, before burying itself at the foot of the nearest cell block. It sat there, half concealed by the ugly concrete, a deadly misshapen green oblong. But Stolcher knew better than to get up a second time, it was clear that the British has installed some sort of delayed fuse on the weapons, presumably to catch people in the open. He buried his face in the yard's cobbles and opened his mouth to await the inevitable.

The blast was epic. The shockwave passed through him, pressing the air out of his lungs, and the consequent explosion robbed him of his hearing momentarily. He was saved from flying debris by the luck of finding himself in the lee of the vehicles, which suffered greatly from the explosive force. No more than the cell block wall, however, which was torn down like a flimsy sheet of wallpaper. When the dust settled, it left a mound of rubble two stories high leading up to the exposed cell blocks above, all of which appeared empty to Stolcher's confused and red-rimmed eyes. Two further explosions sounded on the other side of the thick wall, but neither harmed Stolcher, who rolled onto his back in agony. His ears rang and his breathing was ragged with all the dust carried in the air.

With great pain, he forced himself up into a sitting position. The soldiers of his escort seemed to have disappeared and two of the trucks burned fiercely. It occurred to him that he would almost certainly get the blame for this, too. Then he remembered that it *was* his fault. With a bitter smile, he reflected that the whereabouts of S.O.E.'s agents could only have become known to the woman he had imprisoned here and then allowed to escape. Eve Moore, he reminded himself. If he survived this, he would certainly ensure that she paid dearly for this humiliation.

Concussion had set in, so he was only half-conscious of the arrival of a third aircraft. It was quieter in comparison to the other two and he gazed up at it as it made its approach, almost like time itself had slowed down. Its wheels extended below the wings and this prompted a hysterical laugh. He shouted up at the aeroplane, 'What now? Are you going to land on the Champs Elysee and come fetch me yourselves?'

His question was answered a matter of seconds later when the prison's gatehouse disappeared in a spectacular flash. It sent masonry flying in all directions and was instantly replaced by a cloud of grey smoke and dust. Something grazed Stolcher's forehead and everything went black. When he came to, he saw through blurry eyes dark figures emerging from the pall surrounding the ruined gate. Some fired wildly with sub-machine guns as they ran, still others brandished rifles. These were not the rigid and precise movements of German soldiers; they were irregulars. And no-one in the courtyard stood against them, they sent all before them running or flailing in their path. As Stolcher's vision faded again, he realised that the long-awaited storm had come at last.

*

Peter pushed the throttles forward to the stops. But not through the gate because that would demand engine boost at a penalty to engine life. He wanted everything the machine had to climb quickly. Altitude was precious in an aerial scrap, but he also wanted a reserve because so too was power. He was impressed with the Mosquito's performance, although like a man who tires of his wife after long years of marriage, the longer he spent in the cockpit the more likely he was to find fault with the aircraft. He shook his head – was he so much of an old hand now that he could find himself wishing for a little extra speed from those engines, or that the controls were slightly less heavy when throwing it around?

Charlie appeared from the nose section looking pale and unsteady, as if he'd had a fright. But Peter could not recall anything he'd done that was less than gentle in his approach or climb out.

'Good hit,' Peter said, when Charlie had plugged into the intercom.

'Really? It looked just about dead-on when I punched the tit. The low airspeed was quite helpful to be honest.'

'I caught sight of people on the ground. Looks like Victor's lot made it through, although god knows how many they'll get out after that wall collapsed.'

'Yes.'

'Are you alright? You look a bit fragile.'

'I'm fine. Just a touch unsteady. After last night.'

Peter was sceptical about that. He'd seen Charlie hungover before and this was not it. But it wasn't something he intended to probe; Charlie could be a closed book. As can we all, he reminded himself.

Charlie passed a course correction that would bring them out of France just east of Dunkirk and fell silent. Other than the drone of the engines, which was muffled by his leather flying helmet, Peter luxuriated in blissful isolation. He had begun to consider what Eve's pregnancy meant for him only lately because of the excitement surrounding the operation. In truthfulness, he felt odd about becoming a father since his own childhood had been so unhappy. He felt a renewed desire to finally confront his own father, if only to clear his nagging anxiety that he would turn out like the drunken bully who had put his mother in an early grave. Charlie's voice crackled in his earphones.

'Look out, ten o'clock low. Smoke trail.'

Peter craned his head to look over the coming and caught sight of a twin-engine aircraft several thousand feet below them with a long curving trail of smoke emanating from one of its engines. His keen eye also spotted a smaller shape climbing up and away from it, a fighter.

'It's got to be one of ours,' Peter said. 'Let's get stuck in.'

'Wait a second. What are you going to do, ram him? We've got no guns, remember? You just dropped the only offensive weapons this aircraft carries.'

Peter had in fact forgotten that the aircraft had neither guns nor cannons, but immediately added it to his list of gripes about the B Mk IV variant.

'We can't leave him to be picked off by that Jerry.'

'Where there's one fighter, there's likely to be more. We'll just get ourselves killed.'

'Charlie, I'm not leaving one of our boys to die.'

'"Our boys"? Are you out of your mind? We're not even part of 105 Sq-'

Whatever Charlie was going to say next was lost as Peter rolled the aircraft over on its back and pulled sharply back until the nose pointed at the stricken bomber. He rolled the wings level in the dive and pushed the throttle through the gate, kicking in the supercharger boost. They closed the distance in less than a minute. It felt like free-falling in a lift. Peter did not glance once at the airspeed indicator because he was too scared to see what it read.

When they were about a mile away, he was able to make a more fulsome appreciation of the situation. The damaged aircraft was indeed one of theirs, A-Apple flown by Merrick. Where Dubicki had got to was anybody's guess. A few hundred yards behind it, an unknown German fighter was manoeuvring to take a shot. It was not one that Peter recognised. Certainly not a Me109, for he would have clocked it instantly from the few one-sided encounters he'd had in Blenheims. This thing had a much beefier nose and a long canopy that gave the pilot a much better all-round view. It was probably the new Focke-Wulf 190A that they'd been told about, he concluded. Ironically, Peter smiled, the pilot was not taking advantage of that long canopy because he was too busy lining up to deal Merrick the death blow.

Peter's mind worked quickly and logically to assess the situation and decide upon the best course of action. There were no other fighters around to provide top-cover for this aircraft and, considering his inattention, this pilot was likely inexperienced or possibly out of his depth. A plan hatched in his mind.

'I'm going to try to draw him away to give Merrick the chance to escape,' Peter said.

'And how are you going to do that?'

'Watch.'

Peter had not sacrificed much airspeed in the final furlong and now he applied rudder to slip the aircraft so that its course converged with that of the Focke-Wulf's. He gambled that the pilot would catch him in his peripheral vision as he neared. He did so, although much later than Peter expected. In the instant before they crossed overhead, Peter saw him look up and his expression of absolute terror as he realised he was for it, then the fighter flashed below and behind.

'Jesus, Peter. I thought you were going to collide with him. Our propellors must have missed his canopy by inches.'

'That's just the half of it. Now we need him to chase us.'

It was a huge gamble, that the German would disengage from an advantageous fight against a damaged opponent to attack a perfectly serviceable one. And one that had already caught him out once before. It was a gamble that was born somewhere in Peter's gut, from a set of biases he had developed unknowingly over the past year of operational flying and more than a little natural cunning. As Peter pulled the aircraft into a climb to gain crucial height, he glanced over his shoulder and saw that the gamble had paid off. Jerry had taken the bait.

'Oh, perfect,' Charlie said with a shake of his head. 'Now what?'

Peter pushed the throttle forward to the stops once more and pulled back on the column firmly. The earth disappeared below the cockpit windows and all that could be seen beyond the nose was clear, blue sky.

'Give me the altimeter readings please,' Peter said.

'8,000 feet...9,000 feet,' Charlie called in a neutral voice. 'He's gaining, you know.'

Peter knew he would, the fighter must have better climbing performance than the twin-engine bomber, but he also knew that he had started the race from an unequal footing. They'd had at least 350 mph on the clock when they bounced the fighter, and the German had been doing much less than that when it took up the pursuit. The time it had taken him to develop the speed he had over the bomber meant even more distance between them.

'11,000 feet...12,000. Come on, you can climb faster than this.'

Peter knew Charlie was right, he could climb faster than the 2,000 feet per minute shown by the rate of climb indicator. But he needed to draw the German away from Merrick to enable him to break away. If it was clear that the RAF intruder was never to be caught, the fellow might lose heart and circle back for the easy kill. It was a finely balanced judgement. Too finely balanced, he decided, when the fighter opened up from astern sending cannon rounds slicing past their cockpit.

'17,000, Peter I hope you've got something planned here.'

'Just bear with me,' Peter murmured, easing the stick back to steepen the climb. He was sweating profusely in expectation that another burst of cannon fire would come smashing through the airframe at any moment, effectively ending their escape.

How much longer can this chap keep going for, he asked himself.

The fatal burst did not come. Peter risked a look away from the instruments and saw that the German was marginally further back than he had been moments before. There was a final, impotent burst of fire from longer range that went much wider. He heard Charlie's intonation in his ears as they passed 24,000 feet and the little fighter was still holding on, but had narrowed to little more than a dot. At 28,000 feet their opponent finally broke, yawing off first one way and then the other as the fighter's performance at high altitude counted against him. He had obviously decided that there was little point in continuing the chase now and, as Peter lowered the Mosquito's nose and set up for cruise, he saw that they were well over the Channel.

Perhaps not home and safe, but certainly safer.

The wheels touched down on the dry grass at RAF Swanton Morley less than 35 minutes later. The other two Mosquitoes were already parked up on the dispersal, a fire tender was in attendance. For a secret mission, there was quite a crowd around the assembled aircraft and Peter could not help but feel a tad triumphant as he descended the ladder to shake hands with the beaming Merrick, Dubicki, and the others.

'We did it,' Peter grinned.

'We certainly did, thanks to you and Charlie. That was some show back there, old chap,' Merrick replied. A few others pressed in to ask questions and jostle them around, good-naturedly. Peter used this excitement to quietly extricate himself from the throng and look for Charlie, who stood to one side and stared at him.

'What's wrong? You're not feeling sore about that Focke-Wulf, are you?'

'Peter, I couldn't give a fig about the Focke-Wulf. I've just received this,' Charlie waved a telegram in his hand.

‘What is it?’

‘The news is a few months’ old now. Look, there’s no easy way to say this,’ Charlie began.

‘Just say it, come on.’

‘Your father’s dead. An air raid in Plymouth. It looks like a direct hit on an air raid shelter, no-one made it out alive. I’m so sorry, Peter.’

Peter took the telegram and stared at it, but the longer he looked the less it seemed to make sense. Charlie placed a reassuring hand on his shoulder, but all Peter felt was numbness.

Chapter Eighteen

The rain tapped gently but insistently on the panes of glass, reminding Eve that the summer was at an end and now came the autumn, always too soon. It was a rotten time of year to be in London and she looked forward to retreating to her snug little cottage. But first there were some loose ends to be tied up.

The creak of floorboards outside was a sign that one of those loose ends was about to arrive home shortly. There was a scrape of a key in the lock and then a shaft of light fell across the living room as the door swung open. It slammed, the light went on and Captain Alex Kingham strode into the room. He'd been drinking, of course. She could smell stale beer on him from the doorway in which she'd stood for most of the 50 minutes that had elapsed since breaking into his flat in Victoria.

He jumped when he caught sight of her, 'Who the devil are you?'

'My name's Evelyn Moore. Please sit down.'

'Who let you into my damned flat? What do you mean by this?'

'Oh, do be quiet. I really don't want a fuss. I need to talk to you and the next few minutes are going to be critical, so I caution you to answer me fully and honestly. Why are you working for the Germans?'

If the question resonated with Kingham, he didn't show it. His face wrinkled up into a mask of denial.

'What? This is preposterous, get out before I call the police.'

'You've been working for a German counter-intelligence officer called Erich Stolcher. You gave him direct access to S.O.E. information that permitted him to penetrate an intelligence network and then use that network to mislead us.

Dozens of agents and their helpers ended up being tortured and imprisoned by the Gestapo and several of them were executed. I want to know why.'

Kingham gave her a dangerous look, but said nothing.

'I have witness evidence that says you interfered with F-Section's own wireless procedures. We could have had you arrested and put on trial. But that would only end in one outcome and, quite frankly, the war effort could do with a little less bad news at the moment. So, I'll ask you again, why betray us?'

His eyes darted to the nearby desk and then back to Eve. She saw it and as she took a step towards him, he bounded across the room and pulled a pistol from the top drawer, cocking it as he did so.

'I think our discussion is at an end. Any last questions?'

'You think I didn't turn over your flat when I arrived?'

'You're lying,' Kingham said, but sweat beaded on his forehead. Eve was impressed, it was the first sign of doubt he'd exhibited since he walked in.

'Try me.'

The pistol gave a dead man's click as the firing pin was sent forward. Kingham did not look down to see if any of the other chambers were filled; he knew they were not. Seeing the surprise on his face, Eve pulled her own pistol from her coat.

'I also took the little stiletto knife from beneath your pillow. You're quite heavily armed for an office wallah. Were you expecting trouble?'

Kingham sagged into a leather chair and in a resigned voice said, 'It seems you hold all the cards now, so what do you want to know?'

'Why?'

'Jesus, why not? We're not going to win this war, the Germans are. They're unstoppable on all fronts. They cleared us out of France and they're doing a damned fine job of clearing up the Mediterranean too. When Rommel reaches Suez, it'll all be over and we'll have to sue for peace. And then people like me, who've admired their drive and ambition from afar, we'll get the plum jobs in the newly occupied territories.'

'And Jones helped you?'

'Ivor? God no. Poor old Ivor hadn't a clue that he was being crossed. You know, he taught me Classics at Oxford? One of the bloodiest subjects in the college, always selling each other out or seeing their enemies off, the ancients were. But Ivor was so pleased to be part of our little spy games that he had no idea he was being played himself.'

'Who recruited you?'

'Stolcher. Before the war. He was just some grubby little policeman then, but he had big plans. He became a Party man, not because he believed in what the Nazis said, but because he could see the opportunities opening for capable people without connections. Every cause needs its foot soldiers. How did you find out it was me, anyway?'

'Signals intelligence. You told the girls at Bletchley to ignore the lack of security checks. That was stupid.'

'I had to. They were too damned clever by half; they knew something was up with the Grapple traffic. Typically, the Germans couldn't make it look realistic even though they put their cleverest people on it. People who don't make mistakes. What about Stolcher, does he know he's blown?'

'I'd say so,' Eve said, permitting herself a faint smile. 'Are there others working for the Krauts like you?'

'Oh, come now. That's lazy isn't it? If I tell you all my secrets, then you don't need me at all. No debriefing. No offer to double-cross the Germans. At least work for it: make me an offer,' Kingham flashed her the smile of a man whose opinion is unassailable.

Eve pulled the trigger. Kingham was thrown backwards by the impact of the bullet. Slumped against the wall with a dark patch spreading across his battledress jacket, his last expression was one of complete surprise. Eve rubbed the pistol down with her handkerchief and tossed it into Kingham's lap. It wasn't the most convincing suicide, but she knew people in Special Branch. She checked to ensure the hallway was empty and turned back for a last look at Kingham's body.

'You're right. I wouldn't need you at all.'

*

'Cheers.'

The cork left the bottle with a satisfying pop and flew across the small bistro where it was caught by one of the waiters, to polite applause from the other diners. It was a packed little restaurant, Eve had suggested it when they arranged to meet. The kind of place where, in this time of nationwide rationing, champagne and lobster could still be found for those whose pockets were deep enough to pay for it. Evidently, there were quite a few of those. Peter surveyed the room as he filled four glasses and recognised two politicians and an air vice-marshal amongst the chatty crowd.

It had been quite a day, he reflected, only an hour before he had stood nervously with Charlie in a capacious drawing room in St. James's Palace awaiting a special guest. The King himself, George VI, looked smaller in person than he appeared in the newsreels and the papers, but he had donned his RAF uniform for this special, discreet ceremony. His equerry bore two medal boxes containing the purple and white-ribboned D.F.C., which he pinned onto their tunics in turn. In his soft voice he apologised saying, 'I regret terribly that your awards will never appear in the Gazette but do be assured that the Empire is grateful for your service.'

Peter could not stop looking at the ribbon. Jumbo Sutherland, recently discharged from hospital and confined to a wheelchair, raised his glass and took a deep sip.

'Delightful stuff, I've missed it more than I care to mention. Congratulations on your decorations – "win 'em and wear 'em", that's what I say.'

'There's also something else to celebrate,' Peter replied, looking at his watch and wondering where Eve had got to. 'Charlie, you look miles away. Are you thinking about your French maiden?

'What? Oh, hardly.' Charlie sipped his champagne and looked sideways at Sutherland, 'I was just thinking about that file we retrieved from France. Was it of any use?'

Jumbo cleared his throat and leaned towards them in a conspiratorial fashion. Charlie leaned forwards too.

'No.'

Sutherland laughed deeply at Charlie's confused look, so that a lady at the table behind looked pointedly at him. 'Oh dear, my poor hip. Sorry madam, you'll forgive a convalescent.'

'Come on, don't pull my leg,' Charlie said.

'Oh, alright. All the papers in the dossier you picked up refer to a German special project codenamed *ZINNMAN*.'

'Tinman?'

'That's correct, Peter. The project is a special weapon, some kind of rocket-powered aircraft,' Sutherland lowered his voice, 'The boffins looked over the plans and they've judged it to be legitimate. But the intelligence only provides us with part of the picture. We still don't know for what purpose the weapon is being developed, how advanced the project is, or even where the Germans are testing it.'

'You mean to tell me- wait,' Charlie cocked his head to one side.

'What is it?'

'It's the damnedest thing, I thought I heard a gunshot. Didn't you?'

'I can't hear anything over the sound of that bloody piano. What is that anyway?'

'It's jazz, Jumbo,' Peter replied drily and then turned to Charlie. 'A what?'

'Never mind, it was likely a car backfiring. Jumbo, I was going to ask you about that weapon.'

'I don't think now is quite the time. Why don't you pop by my office tomorrow for a cup of tea? I might need some extra help now that I'm...temporarily *hors de combat.*'

'You're never back at work already?'

'Hey, that's my navigator you're trying to poach there,' Peter cried with equal surprise and chagrin.

'Neither of you have an appointment after your exploits at Fresnes,' Sutherland said, holding up his hands. 'Which was an absolute coup by the way. So, no harm, no foul. Anyway, if I were you, Peter, I'd be spending all my time with this beautiful creature.'

Peter followed Sutherland's gaze as Eve breezed in through the dark curtains masking the door. Recognising the three of them she smiled and waved as Peter and Charlie stood to greet her.

'I'm terribly sorry for keeping you all, it's so difficult to find a cab anywhere outside Westminster these days. Have you ordered? Ooh, champagne – what are we celebrating?'

'Well, there is the small matter of these gongs,' Charlie said, indicating to his chest.

'I've said it before, you're both very clever.' Charlie looked marginally disappointed at Eve's response.

'I'm so pleased to be here with you all this evening,' Peter said, conscious of a formal tone in his voice. 'We've shared such adventures. And especially Eve, who we've recently learned is carrying our child-'

‘Sssssh, Peter,’ Eve said, glancing about.

Peter had rehearsed this several times, but in the critical moment he blurted it out like an idiot, ‘Evelyn Moore, will you marry me?’

Eve gave Peter a kind look but said nothing. Charlie cleared his throat and studied his glass. Sutherland became interested in something happening across the room. Peter felt the dread of embarrassment descend upon him like a wet coat. He knew he’d played a false note, he just didn’t know how. He swallowed hard and tried to pretend no-one was watching. Something deep in his subconscious reminded him that this was a bad idea. Now look what’s happened, it said.

‘Perhaps,’ Eve began, ‘Perhaps, Peter, I might have a word outside for just a moment, please?’

Outside on the dark street, a few late-night partygoers tottered past towards Horseferry Road, otherwise it was quiet.

‘I know that this was hardly what you expected, Peter. It was hardly what I expected either. And I appreciate that you are doing the thing you believe to be correct and honourable-’

Eve gripped the lapels of his jacket and looked into his eyes, ‘But I don’t want to marry you. Please, listen to me. I don’t want to marry anyone; I won’t be someone’s wife and give up doing what I love.’

Peter ran a hand through his thick hair, he had no idea what to say.

‘I love you, Peter. I want us to bring up our child together and I want you to know that there is no one else in my heart but you. I know this will be confusing for you, you dear sweet thing, but I hope you’ll understand it doesn’t change anything. What’s a marriage anyway? It’s just a silly piece of paper.’

‘Darling,’ Peter replied in a voice that sounded different to his own, ‘Of course you’re right. Marriage is so old hat; as long as I have you, I couldn’t be happier.’

It was a smiling Eve that led Peter by the hand back to the table. As she did so, Peter told himself that he could change her mind. It would require time and effort, but he knew that he could bring her round eventually and they would live a long and happy life together. He too was smiling by the time he caught Charlie's curious look, so that his friend placed his cigarette between his lips and started a ragged applause that was picked up by people at the tables closest to them.

'Here's to the happy couple,' Charlie said.

'Delighted for you both,' Sutherland cried, slapping Peter's forearm.

'Well, just before you tell the whole of London, I should be clear that Eve has kindly agreed *not* to marry me. So, please raise your glasses in a toast to *staying true to one another*.'

'I say,' Sutherland replied, 'That's a damned fine toast; I'll drink to that.'

Unsure of whether it was the drink, or the ambience, in the cramped little restaurant in Victoria, Peter watched his friends talk and roar with laughter at their stupid jokes or tall tales with a growing feeling of comfort. Their faces were lit by the modest flames of the cheap tallow candles that threw great shadows on the walls behind them, which danced and shimmied as they joined with those from a dozen other tables. It was September 1941, a dreadful year for the forces of good. But Peter realised that, though here and now the darkness unquestionably outweighed its opposing element, in some places the light still managed to shine through.

Author's Note

A popular hypothetical question is whether 1941 or 1942 was a worse year for Great Britain's war effort. What is certain is that 1941 was truly a dark time. It must have seemed like a series of disappointing setbacks and reversals as first Greece and Crete fell (although crucially Malta held out), the Germans launched unrestricted submarine warfare in the Atlantic, and the Afrika Corps arrived in Tunisia. But by the end of the year, Winston Churchill had some cause for optimism. For one thing, he had gained allies. Both the U.S.S.R. and the United States of America officially joined the war with the Axis powers. Second, in the RAF, the Prime Minister had the means to strike directly at the heart of Nazi Germany. Its activities might be a controversial topic for some, but Bomber Command's operations drained fighting strength and forced Germany to invest in air defences.

I had the idea for *The Night Service* when I was still writing the first in the series and found myself scribbling ideas for scenes and characters in the margins of editing that debut novel. I was keen to write a sort of homage to the work of the RAF that occurred out of sight of the public eye. It was inspired by three real life incidents that occurred during the Second World War, although I changed times and places to fit this story.

The first was the *Englandspiel*, a deception operation played against S.O.E.'s Dutch (N-Section) bureau between 1942-44 by an Abwehr agent named Hermann Giskes. Giskes captured a couple of Dutch agents that had been blind-dropped into the Netherlands and was able to use false wireless messages to convince S.O.E. that they were building an intelligence network worthy of investment. Ignoring their own security protocols,

S.O.E. subsequently dropped 52 more agents almost directly into the hands of the waiting Germans. It was only the RAF's intervention when they realised their aircraft were getting shot down only on their way *back* from operations that eventually halted the game.

Similar to the *Englandspiel*, the destruction of Major Francis Suttill's Prosper Network in 1943 showed S.O.E. at its absolute worse. Lax security protocols and poor local operational security, not to mention a double agent named Henri Dericourt, led to the network's demise. Shamefully, it appeared that British agents warned the head of F-Section, Maurice Buckmaster, about Dericourt's betrayal and were ignored. If you wish to know more about these incidents, then I can recommend Kate Vigurs' *Mission France: The True History of the Women of SOE* and Leo Marks' *Between Silk and Cynanide: A Codemaker's War*, 1941-1945 (there are countless others too).

Finally, the RAF's daring raid on Amiens Prison, known as Operation JERICHO, encouraged me to draw the book to a close in a manner that I hope is a tribute to the planning and execution of that mission. The real operation saw 18 Mosquitos from 467, 464 and 21 squadrons strike their target at low level to enable the Resistance to free nearly 80 detainees and political prisoners. It also resulted in the sad loss of Group Captain Percy Pickard D.S.O. (and two bars), D.F.C., star of the film *Target For Tonight* and a former commanding officer of 161 (Special Duties) Squadron.

For more on the less well-known aspects of the RAF's Special Duties squadrons, I would advise reading *We Landed by Moonlight: The Secret RAF Landings in France 1940-1944* by Hugh Verity. Verity flew as a pick-up pilot with 161 Squadron at the height of the war and his book is excellent for putting you in the cockpit at the heart of the action. It provides a wealth of detail about the risks these very brave men ran to keep resistance alive. I hope that Verity, et al, will forgive me for plundering their operational record for inspiration in this book.

I have to admit to being somewhat 'flexible' with the history in order to ensure the storyline flows freely. Readers will appreciate that 105 Squadron only really began the process of converting onto the Mosquito B Mk. IV in November (not September as represented here) 1941 and was not truly operational until September 1942. Equally, RAF Special Duties operations reached their peak in 1943, with only a handful of missions being flown in the period 1940-41. I've also given S.O.E. a bit of a hard time in the book, but I think deservedly. Whilst S.O.E. was a product of its time, it feels all too often it sent people to do a job that they were not prepared or equipped to undertake. Its amateurish approach was responsible for many untimely deaths. Its rivalry with MI6 was certainly not a matter of fiction and more on this can be found in *MI6: The History of the Secret Intelligence Service 1909-1949* by Keith Jeffery.

I'm always keen to hear readers' thoughts and ideas on my work. You can email me at tomwalker188d@outlook.com or visit my website www.tomwalkerauthor.com where you can subscribe to my mailing list for updates on the Wings of Victory series or read my blog. Whether things got better in 1942 remains a matter of conjecture. For Peter and Charlie, the war continues.

Acknowledgements

I was humbled by the support I received from friends, colleagues, and fellow writers in bringing *The Night Service* to life. I must thank my mum and dad, my brother Oliver, and Izzy & Freddie for their patience, reassurance and understanding over the long and irregular hours spent researching, typing, and reading. A huge debt of gratitude also goes to my partner, Aly Balsom, for her advice and support – she remains my real-life Evelyn Moore.

Thanks are also due to a group of people who have helped, encouraged, or just provided an ear from time to time. There are so many that I cannot name everyone, but special mention goes to: Alan Greenwood, Matt Symons, Rob McCartney, Sam Fletcher, Sir Barney White-Spunner, Nicholas Lezard, Frank Barnard, Jo Thoenes and Robert Adam.

Finally, I owe a big thank you to my publisher, Richard Foreman, and the team at Sharpe Books for transforming my manuscript into something that people can actually read. As ever, any mistakes are entirely mine

Printed in Great Britain
by Amazon

33595928R00128